DUTY BOUND

BOOK ONE OF THE ANGELBOUND LINCOLN SERIES

CHRISTINA BAUER

D1678290

COPYRIGHT

Monster House Books
Brighton, MA 02135
ISBN 9781946677198
First Edition

CONTENTS

APPENDIX

DEDICATION

For All Those Who Kick Ass, Take Names
and Read Books

AUTHOR NOTE

Dear Readers,

Forty-eight months and a million years ago, I outlined the story of Lincoln *before* he met Myla ... a tale that became DUTY BOUND.

Key fact: If you're hungering for Lincoln's voice *in tandem with* some serious Myla interaction, then there's book 2 in this series, LINCOLN.

But I digress.

Back to DUTY BOUND.

In the years since ANGELBOUND was released, I've been thrilled by the ongoing love for all things Lincoln and Myla. My readers even voted to have Lincoln's story told—and since I love to make readers happy—here it is!

I hope you enjoy it :)

Christina Bauer

AUTHOR NOTE PART DEUX

Dear Readers,

This note contains my suggested reading order for all things Angelbound. So if you want to skip ahead to that part, feel free! Bottom line: I'm a non-linear thinker and my books sometimes come out in an odd order. I try to stop this, but then the writing stops. Eek. That said, let's get to the good stuff.

My Suggested Angelbound Reading Order

Below please find the suggested reading order for my current Angelbound titles:

1. ANGELBOUND
2. DUTY BOUND (Book 1 in the new Lincoln POV series)

3. LINCOLN (Book 2 in the new Lincoln POV series)

4. SCALA

5. ACCA and the rest of the current Angelbound Origins series

6. The current Angelbound Offspring series (*MAXON* Special Edition and so on)

In case you're wondering, I still plan to release books about Xavier, Cissy and Walker. However, Author Me needs to get more Lincoln POV novels out of my head first. In the meantime, I hope you enjoy all things Angelbound!

Thanks (again!) for reading and being you,

Christina

DUTY BOUND

I am Lincoln Vidar Osric Aquilus, High Prince of the Thrax. My people are renowned as the greatest demon hunters across Heaven, Hell, Earth, Purgatory, and the Dark Lands. At eighteen years old, I've killed precisely one thousand four hundred and thirty-seven demons in hand-to-hand combat, more than any other thrax in history. All of which leads to a single inescapable conclusion.

I can make it through this breakfast with my mother.

At least, I think I can.

"You haven't touched your eggs, my son." Mother spears a strawberry off her plate. After many years of maternal encounters, I've learned to keep my mouth closed in situations like this one. Mother will bring up her true concerns when she's good and ready.

In reply, I merely maintain her stare. We've an odd relationship, but a close one. We're both natural schemers, so neither wants to pass up a test of intelligence and charm.

"Perhaps you dislike formal breakfasts," says Mother as she gestures to my tunic.

"I'm fine with wearing royal garb to meals. Rest assured, all my Batman costumes are safely packed away." As a child, I fought hard to dress as a human superhero. Unlike demon killing, that was one battle I ultimately lost.

"So you say." A small smile rounds Mother's mouth. "Those tunics hide quite a lot."

"True. I've a Bohemian Rhapsody T-shirt on under this thing."

"I have no idea what that is, but I'm pleased to see you turned out so well."

This morning, I'm dressed in a velvet tunic, leather pants, and tall boots. Meanwhile, Mother looks regal and lethal in her black velvet gown. She has porcelain skin, delicate features, and an all-knowing glare that reduces hardened warriors to mush.

Needless to say, I'm pleased that her glare has softened. I must remember to work Batman into our conversations more often.

For a few minutes, Mother and I continue our breakfast in silence. It would be pleasant, except for the setting. Our new feasting hall is located in Purgatory.

Yes, Purgatory.

This place combines the worst of a rundown human suburb with the best of a rotting Dumpster. The sky is constantly cloudy with two types of weather: rainy and about to rain. It's part of the magic of this realm that the weather is always dreary. Plus, the sky never reveals the sun or moon, and even if it did, those celestial bodies follow different patterns than they do in other realms.

Closing my eyes, I let my thoughts return to the glittering caverns of my homeland. As a rule, thrax live underground on Earth in the realm of Antrum. For some reason, the oracle angel, Verus, has demanded the royal family—and our noble entourage—move to Purgatory for a short period of time. This wasn't a popular idea, but the oracle's word is law, so we arrived here three months ago. Until Verus sets us loose, our days will be spent in tents and wooden halls like this one.

I scan the empty benches around me and sigh. It's hard being separated from the bulk of my people. Quiet breakfasts like this only make things worse. Usually our feasting hall is packed with thrax sharing breakfast at communal tables. However, today Mother insisted on having a family-only morning meal, which in this case translates into me, Mother, and a half-dozen terrified workers. Father should arrive any minute now. I can only hope he arrives before Mother's temper returns.

As if in reply to my thoughts, Mother spears another wilted strawberry with a vengeance. Looks like her temper will resurface before Father does. Bugger.

"You never answered my question," says Mother "You haven't touched your food." She spears a grape with such force the entire table wobbles.

"Careful there," I say. "You'll bring down the roof down."

"One perk of being queen. I can bring down roofs and no one says a thing."

At those words, the half-dozen servants in the room visibly shiver.

There's no question about the general topic of Mother's angst, either. It's always the same issue: the House of Acca. That tribe is the largest and most troublesome of all thrax.

At this point, problems with Acca could fall into one of two categories.

One, Mother might be worried about my impending marriage contract with Acca's most eligible noblewoman, Lady Adair. If Mother thinks there are problems on that front, she would be sorely mistaken. It's a business arrangement, nothing more. I'd regret that, but I'm a prince. I always knew I'd never marry for love.

Two—and far more worrisome—would be if Mother discovered my ongoing scheme against Aldred, the dreaded Earl of Acca himself. I've many issues with the earl, but my largest is how Aldred keeps leading his warriors into ill-planned demon attacks on the Earth's surface. Thanks to the Earl of Acca, hundreds of good thrax meet bad ends every week. I meet with the families of the fallen, trying to provide comfort as their worlds fall apart. So many tears and ruined lives…and all so the earl can prove his so-called prowess in battle.

It's outrageous.

Even worse, my parents have forbidden me from doing anything to stop Aldred's bloodshed. Per some ancient treaty, if I interfere with Aldred's rights to lead his troops, then the earl has the unmitigated right to execute me on the spot.

And as every royal knows, execution threats and breakfast do not mix well.

Mother narrows her eyes. Like all thrax, she has mismatched irises, one brown and the other blue. "Answer the question, child. Why aren't you eating?"

I stare at my plate of runny scrambled eggs. "Not hungry." I'm not much of a foodie on any occasion, but the royal menu has taken a serious nosedive ever since we moved to Purgatory. This realm doesn't even have cable, let alone the ability to run power lines to our campground. All things considered, the royal chef's doing wonders with mobile stoves and Bunsen burners.

Mother waves at the roomful of servants. "Leave us." A half-dozen thrax in traditional medieval garb skitter from the room. The queen is in a mood, and they all know it.

Sadly, I can't escape so easily.

Mother daintily pats the corners of her mouth with a white linen napkin. "I'm quite concerned about Acca."

And here it is.

Mother is ready to confront me, and hopefully not about the topic of execution. With a force of will, I keep my features calm. "And what about Acca?"

"You…" She pins me with another withering gaze. Mother can always sense when I'm hiding something.

Unfortunately for me, I am.

"Me…" I say slowly. "You're about to say how wonderful I am, right? Running the government, fighting demons? You couldn't wish for a finer prince." Normally, this reply gets me a half-smile at least.

Not this morning.

Mother leans back on her bench, and I can almost picture the gears of her mind whirring overtime. "You're an excellent son. That's not what concerns me." Her nostrils flare. "You danced with Lady Adair at the ball last night."

I shrug. "I danced with a number of noblewomen. Adair didn't receive any special attention."

"I wish I could believe that. Do you..." Mother inhales a shaky breath. "Do you *love* her, Lincoln?"

Oh, that.

My parents have always been a united front on the "no love in royal marriage" rule. For my mother's part, I know it's because she and father continue to battle over Acca. She sees love as her weakness; it makes her give in to Father on all things Aldred. She's not wrong, either. That's why I've never fought that particular rule. Nothing like watching years of your parents sparring to convince you to sidestep the love part of "love and marriage."

Father is a different story. I never have been able to figure out why he's so dead set against my falling in love. Eventually, after years of trying to suss it out, I've given up on the subject. I agree with them both and that's all that matters.

"So you wish to know if I love Lady Adair." I shrug. "How can I? I barely know her. By all accounts, she seems a fine woman, and I'm sure she'll make a competent queen. We'll grow to respect each other with time. That's more than enough."

This is the mantra I've been raised on. Still, saying the words out loud always makes something in my chest tighten. There's nothing to be done about it, however. It's not like I've met any woman who would tempt me in that regard anyway. Some men simply aren't built for love.

Mother visibly slumps with relief. "Excellent. Emotion has no place in royal marriages, my child. You know how I adore your father, but when it comes to ruling, love only adds unnecessary levels of complexity."

"I know, Mother. Believe me."

I glance toward the door. Speaking of unnecessary levels of complexity, Father is late for breakfast, even by his lax standards. Every morning, my father has an early and extended walk with Aldred. Tension coils up my spine. I can only hope the earl hasn't discovered my secret plans. Recently, I secretly borrowed a few rather incriminating books from his library. If Aldred finds that out—and shares the news with Father—then my scheme could fall apart. More lives would be lost, including mine.

"Lincoln?"

"Yes, Mother?"

"What were you thinking of just now?"

Damn. My concern must have shown. "Nothing at all, unless you count contemplating how agreeable it is to share breakfast with my dear mother."

"Bah. I'm being perfectly gruesome, and you know

it." Mother taps her pointer finger against the side of her teacup. "You're hiding something from me."

"Everyone needs to have secrets. You taught me that."

She leans forward. "So you *are* developing an attachment to Adair."

This is growing tiresome.

"No, I'm not."

"How I wish I could be certain."

Mother and I share yet another long look. We both have the same analytical nature. Together, she and I essentially run Antrum. Most times, the job is fatiguing but manageable...except when Father injects himself into the mix. And Father only does that when the House of Acca is involved. Quite sadly, Acca involves themselves quite a lot.

Here's the crux of the challenge with Acca. They're the only house *not* under the direct rule from the crown. It's all because my house, Rixa, broke away from Acca and took their throne. At the time, granting Acca some autonomy seemed the gracious thing to do. That was five hundred years ago. Today, that autonomy makes Acca nothing but a pain in my backside. All of which is why a closer alliance with them is necessary. Marrying into Acca will give me more control over that unruly house.

Unfortunately, it won't allow me to stop the Earl of

Acca from leading his warriors to their doom. That's where my scheming comes into play. In a matter of days, the waning moon rises. Acca calls it the Archer's Moon. According to my research, there's a rare Acca tradition associated with that occurrence, and if I work things out correctly, I can use it to break Aldred's hold on his warriors.

Assuming I don't die in the process, that is.

And that I make it through this breakfast.

The main door swings open, hitting the wall with a thud. Father bursts into the room, all burly chest, white hair, and jovial manner. A hive of servants buzzes in behind him. Mother's eyes glitter as her gaze meets his.

Father races up to Mother, pulls her from her bench, and twirls her about. "Morning, Octavia." He nibbles at her neck; she giggles.

For the umpteenth time, I wonder at how Father can promote Acca until Mother is ready to scream with frustration, and yet the next day he's able to sidestep the entire issue with a charming *good morning*. Mother's ability to forgive is a skill all in itself. For better or worse, it's one gift that I didn't inherit.

Most of all, that's why my marriage will be one of convenience, nothing more. I've even started the royal architects on building a new Queen's Wing for our palace. It will be regal, comfortable, and far away from the King's Wing. No need to see one's spouse more often than necessary.

Mother takes Father's hand; their fingers entwine. Then her eyes narrow as she flips his arm behind his back, pinning him to the wall.

"Got you."

"Oh, my. Octavia, you beast!"

"Please. That was far too easy." Mother used to be quite the warrior in her day. Still is. She could kick Father's ass any time she wanted to.

He laughs. "I'm getting soft, I won't deny it." Craning his neck, Father talks over his shoulder at Mother. "You should at least break my arm. Teach me a lesson."

She chortles. "Maybe next time. We head out on our anniversary trip today. I wouldn't want you incapacitated."

Father winks. "How very thoughtful of you."

This is my chance to leave. If I know these two—and I do—then they'll be all cute and cuddly with each other for ten more minutes, minimum. That is, until Father drops his latest bomb from Acca. No doubt, after meeting with the earl this morning, Father is ready to launch yet another long list of unreasonable demands. Hopefully that list doesn't include any sanctions on my secret plans. Some of the books I borrowed cover obscure Acca house laws, including ones that touch on demon patrol. Talk about your red flags. If Aldred discovered those books were missing, they might piece together my true intentions.

All the more reason to exit before the topic arises.

With maximum stealth, I step toward the door, but Mother releases her captive, blocking my path. "Husband, did you notice your son at the ball last night?"

Father shoots me a look and winks once more. "Not at all, my dear. What do they say cloud-side on Earth?" He sets his hand on his chest and starts to sing. "I only had eyes for yooooooou." He lumbers over to one of the tables and pulls a honey roll from a stack, which sends a dozen others tumbling to the floor. The host of servants who followed Father inside now race to put the bread back in place.

Father's wink wasn't lost on Mother. He's had a hundred years of marriage with the Queen of the Poker Face, and yet Father still hasn't learned how to hide a single emotion. Mother purses her lips. "Don't bother playing games with me." She frowns. "Lincoln was dancing overmuch with Adair, as you well know."

Father plunks into a chair and bites into his roll. "I don't think one dance is overmuch."

"We should reinforce that emotion has no place in royal marriages." Mother primly smooths back her hair. "Don't you agree?"

Father finishes another honey roll and licks the sticky sugar off his fingers. "Please. Our son isn't some addlebrained fool about to fall in love. That's right, Lincoln, isn't it?"

"Obviously." Once more, I slip my way closer to the exit. "While I appreciate your collective concern for my emotional well-being, I promised Zachary some pointers on how to keep a good watch."

Father taps his lips. "Zachary?"

"Ormand's son." Mother rattles off facts on her fingertips. "The boy's lineage is three-fourths Rixa, one quarter Gurith. He has the heart of a warrior." Gurith is Mother's house. She openly favors anyone with their bloodline.

"Oh, that's right." Father rubs his whiskered chin. "The lad is eight now, I believe. A little flighty, isn't that so? Draws pictures, too."

I take another step toward the door. *Not far now.* "Flightiness goes along with being young and new to training." All thrax warriors start their training at eight. "And a talent for drawing doesn't mean he won't be a fine warrior one day, either. If you'll excuse me." I wrap my fingers around the wooden handle.

So close.

That's when Father clears his throat. My chest tightens.

No good conversation ever started with Father clearing his throat.

"One more thing," says Father.

I slowly turn around. "Yes?"

"Aldred tells me you've been snooping around his archives."

And there it is. The fact that leads to my secret schemes to keep Aldred from killing his own people. Once again, I keep my demeanor calm. "I may become heir to his house; I should get to know its history."

"Snooping in archives?" Mother straightens her back, and *that's* another warning sign if I ever saw one. "My spy network told me no such thing."

"Even your network has limits, Octavia." Father returns his attention to me. "You took some books, I hear."

"On history." *And other things.*

"Does that history have anything to do with Aldred and his demon patrols, my boy?"

Damn.

Of course, the books I took cover the topic of demon patrol. I won't reveal that to Father, though. Demon patrols are a thrax way of life. Each thrax house takes turns policing the Earth's surface. We ensure that humans are safe and unaware of the many kinds of evil that walk among them. In general, I run all of these missions, except for those led by Acca. Technically, it's during those patrols that Aldred has the right to send his warriors into unnecessary battle.

For now, he does.

I grip my hands behind my back. "I thought we were discussing my impending marriage to Adair."

"Nope, I've changed topics," counters Father. "I don't know what books you stole, but it seems Aldred knows you're concerned about the warriors who perish on his patrols. He's the only earl who is allowed to lead his troops personally. That's a right he'll protect forever, and it won't change with any marriage contract." The lines of Father's face tighten. "He let me know that if anyone threatens that right—anyone at all—then the law says Aldred can execute them."

"I'm aware." *And I'm willing to take the risk.*

"Please be careful," says Mother. "Aldred is positively insane when it comes to his rights over demon patrol. Avoid the topic like the plague. We simply can't lose you."

"And you won't lose me. Ever." Behind my back, I tighten my grip on the handle so hard I'm surprised I don't yank it off the door. "Is there nothing else?"

Mother gives me another classic from her collection of soul-searing looks. "There is, but I'll have to suss it out on my own, it seems." She reseats herself at the table and lifts her teacup.

"Good day to you both." With that, I quickly leave the feasting hall without any further interruptions.

Thank Heaven.

Walking at full speed, I rush off to meet young Zachary in the stables. With every step across the yellowing grasses, my resolve hardens.

Avoid it like the plague, indeed.

Dozens of thrax perish every week due to Aldred's incompetence.

I'm fighting him with everything I've got.

2

*H*ere in Purgatory, the stables are arguably the finest building in the thrax compound. Mostly, thrax life in Purgatory takes place in a network of small and rustic cabins. Not so for our horses. Our stables in Purgatory are a long, low, and rectangular structure made from solid oak. A grassy fields leads up to the building's front gates. Behind the structure, there stretches a relatively lush forest. Even the stable's arched roof is lined with carved filigree.

We thrax love our horses.

I steal across the grounds to the main entrance, careful to open the gated doors without making a sound. Young Zachary is supposed to be on watch up in the hayloft. We've seen some minor demonic activity here, so cadets like Zachary have been placed on watch. It makes for a good training exercise.

Moving silently, I close the gates behind me. Zachary makes no sound, either, which means he's either silently peering at me through the slats of wood above my head or he's taking a nap.

Light snores sound from above me.

Taking a nap it is.

I don't blame him for falling asleep. We put our lads through a tough training schedule. When you're eight years old, it isn't easy to focus for six minutes, let alone stay on watch for six hours. But the shifts are necessary parts of their training. One day, this boy will be a man who fights demons. We set high standards to keep him alive. This is one of the main differences between Acca and Rixa.

I move to stand at the ladder leading up to the loft and clear my throat. The snoring continues. Cupping my hand by my mouth, I state in a loud voice: "Report out, warrior."

That gets a far different reaction.

A chorus of gasps and shuffles come from the hayloft. Within seconds, Zachary has scaled down the ladder and stands before me. He's a tiny and lanky kid in his light leather body armor. All I see are knees, elbows, and big mismatched eyes. He's panting with panic.

"My prince, I'm so sorry. About four hours ago, there were Doxy demons in the stable."

"What class?"

"Green bodies, big heads, and spiky bat wings. These are minor Doxies, so they're a…" Zachary screws up his tongue as he thinks things through. "Class F?"

"Quite right." We thrax rank our demons by letter. Class A's are the toughest. "And what did you do?"

"Since it was Class F, I just observed."

"Right again." So long these are only Class F demons, then we've asked the boys not to fight or send out an alarm. Their mission is merely to observe. You don't get to know your enemy if you kill them within minutes of seeing them. Observing demons is an important part of training, so long as they aren't a threat. Even then, thrax don't kill an enemy unless directly attacked. "What did you do then?"

"I watched them, just like the commander told me to. Plus, I drew some pictures of what I saw. I got so excited and then, I just fell asleep. I'm so, so sorry. You can punish me now." He scrubs his oversize hands down his thin face. This boy will be a tall one someday. "I should never have fallen asleep."

The child is doing such a great job at beating himself up, I can't add in to the mix. "You fell asleep because of the adrenaline crash. It's natural."

"No, it's not natural. It's me. I'm not like the other kids. The watch is really hard for me."

I know what Zachary is talking about. The child is a bundle of energy when he's awake, the kind of kid whose attention flits from one thing to the next. "Some things are harder for you. I understand."

"There's no way I can stand still. I want to be a fighter." His voice cracks when he says this part. "It's not in me, though."

In my army, there's always a place for this kind of passion for service, and I know just how to explain it to this child. I kneel down so I can look him straight on. "When I was your age, do you know what was hard for me?"

Zachary's eyes widen. "Something was hard for you?"

"Surely. For me, it was moving quickly in battle."

"But they say you're so fast, you could catch lighting."

My heart goes out to the lad. About ten years ago, I stood in a stable not so different from this one and had a similar conversation with my father.

"I may be the fastest now, but not when I was your age."

"What did you do?"

"I worked harder and longer until I became as good as anyone else. And then I worked even harder until I got better than all of them. We all have gifts and deficits. The only thing we control is how hard we work. I bet you'll stick to it when it comes to watch. In the end, I wouldn't be surprised if you became the best watchman in your crew."

"Do you really think so?"

"Well, are you willing to work long and hard? I'm talking years and years now."

"Yes, my prince."

"Then I truly believe that it will come to pass." I straighten myself to stand upright again. "Now, I'd like to see those pictures you drew of the Doxies."

"Well, I didn't draw the Doxies." He winces. "I drew the warrior."

"Who?"

"The one who came in and led all the demons away."

My brows lift. Leading a pack of Doxies away? That would be a rather clever trick. Not many thrax would know enough arcane demon lore to pull that one off. "Do you know who it was?"

Zachary keeps shuffling his feet. "I think it was a girl."

"A girl thrax warrior?" The house of Gurith has some young girls who may go into training someday, but other than that, we don't have any active female warriors in Purgatory. It's a point of major frustration for Mother. And for me as well, as a matter of fact. I sometimes wonder if I'd take more interest in the opposite sex if some of them knew how to fight.

And now, Zachary has seen a girl warrior in the stables.

I eye him carefully. "Are you sure?"

"She was wearing ghoul robes, so it was hard to tell."

Purgatory is ruled by ghouls, all of whom are extraordinarily tall and wear long black robes. Around here, it's easy enough to get your hands on a set of ghoul robes, and it would be hard to tell anyone's identity while they were wearing some. Zachary could easily mistake a boy for a girl. Or a ghoul for a thrax, for that matter. "Are you certain this warrior wasn't ghoul-kind?"

"No, she was way too short."

Again, he seems to be convinced the fighter was a girl. "What did she look like?"

"It was too dark to see much, but I saw a little bit. I drew a picture, too."

"May I see it?"

Zachary pulls a scrap of paper from under his leather breastplate. I take it from his hands, unfold it, and see an image that takes my breath away. It's a gorgeous girl, about my age, I'd guess. She wears ghoul robes, but the hood has partly fallen away. I can see her intelligent eyes, even features, and sly smile. Long locks of wavy hair frame her face. Something in my chest tightens.

My breath turns short.

The entire stables take on a hazy look, like I've just stepped into a dream.

I tilt my head. Am I under some kind of magic spell? Not possible. I'm scanned for enchantments regularly. No, this feeling must be a sour stomach from that ill-cooked breakfast. People don't simply glance at a fantasy drawing of a pretend girl from an eight-year-old boy and start having feelings for her. I start handing Zachary back the image. "Thank you," I say. "You're relieved from your post now. You did well."

Zachary starts to take the picture and stops. "You can keep it if you want." He lowers his voice. "I saw how you looked at her. She's really pretty."

I stare at the image in my hand. Perhaps I will keep the drawing, but not because the girl is gorgeous and makes my heart palpitate. More for training purposes only. "Thank you, Zachary. You've a very bright imagination."

His mouth thins. "I didn't make her up. I swear."

I slip the paper under my own tunic and smile. *Why am I grinning?* Stomach problems don't cause smiles. Perhaps I should go and get rechecked for enchantments. "I'm sure you didn't."

As soon as the words leave my mouth, I wish I could take them back. There are no beautiful thrax female warriors running around stables and posing for eight-year-old artists. An idea occurs. Perhaps the boy is the one who got enchanted. Some of the young wizards from the House of Striga like to play pranks like this. That's an item to research for later.

A low hum sounds in the air. Zachary gasps. "What's that?"

"That's the hum of a ghoul portal about to open." Ghouls are incredibly tall, pasty-skinned, and fearsome looking. In general, they aren't too tough in battle. That said, they do have the ability to open portals: door-size holes that allow them to zap from one spot to the other. We've locked the ghouls out of Antrum, for obvious reasons. They could portal in a demon horde if they wanted to. And some are nasty enough to do just that. Even so, here in Purgatory, the ghouls rule the land and go where they like.

"Is it an enemy?" asks Zachary.

I tilt my head and concentrate on the sound. "No."

"How can you tell?"

"Each ghoul has their own tone when they create a portal, and this ghoul is my friend Walker. Remember him? I mentioned him before. He's the warrior and artist."

Zachary steps backward toward the exit archway. All this talk of ghouls definitely has the lad worried. "Did you say I was excused?"

"Ghouls look fearsome, but they're actually rather gentle. And Walker is also the brightest engineer you'll ever meet."

"Oh, I forgot he was your friend." Zachary stops his backward walk. His little knees are visibly knocking together, though. "I'll stay if you want me to, my prince."

What a brave and loyal lad. He'll do well.

"I appreciate the offer, but no, thank you. Your shift is over. Please head home and get some sleep."

Spinning about, Zachary races from the stables so quickly you'd think the place was on fire. I make a mental note to have Walker give some instructional speeches to the new lads. My young thrax warriors need to get used to ghouls in general—and Walker in particular—if they want to rise in my ranks. I trust Walker with my life. He never does anything without a purpose, and he certainly isn't one to pop into stables unannounced for no reason. All of which means that I know one thing for certain.

Walker isn't transporting here for a social call. Something is very wrong indeed.

3

*T*he hum grows louder. A moment later, a large door-shaped black rectangle appears in the stables. Through it steps a ghoul in long black robes. He has a brush cut, white skin, emotive eyes, and stylish sideburns. A moment after the ghoul moves inside, the door-like hole behind him vanishes.

I grin. Walker is here. As my best friend, Walker is the only person I've trusted with the truth about my scheme against Aldred. In fact, he's been tasked with spying on Acca and reporting if Aldred does anything too crazy. As a ghoul, Walker is a neutral party. He's also exceptionally sneaky. The earl still doesn't suspect he's being followed.

"Greetings, Your Highness." Walker scans the stables. "Are we alone?"

"We are." My pulse quickens. "He's at it again, isn't he?"

Walker nods. "The Earl of Acca has taken it upon himself to lead a rather large demon patrol into battle." He lowers his voice. "The Archer's Moon shines tonight on Earth."

"I should have expected this." When the Earth's moon is at its thinnest, it resembles a curved-out bow. Acca are masters of archery, so they call this heavenly body the Archer's Moon. It's a secret tradition for Acca leaders to perform great feats of battle during the Archer's Moon. "What's Aldred doing?"

"He's got a hundred thrax against a single she-demon."

I purse my lips. "Sounds reasonable." *For once.*

"He can't get a read on the demon's class."

A jolt of worry shoots across my shoulders. It's a basic rule of thrax battle training—never engage an enemy until its class is clear. With most demons, you can define their class on sight. Plus, if there's ever a question, the wizards from the House of Striga arm us with divining charms. Even the Earl of Acca can't be so thick as to ignore those protocols. "Let me get this straight. He doesn't know the class, and yet he's still planning to attack?"

"Unfortunately." Walker has very pronounced bone

structure, but I've never seen him look more gaunt or worried. "He's never led this many in one charge before."

"Let's go then."

"Are you certain?" Walker knows the risks.

"Execution threats be damned. I'm not letting even one more thrax die. We're leaving."

"Shouldn't you change into battle armor?" Walker gestures across my formal tunic.

"No time. Can you portal us there?"

"If you're certain."

"Positive."

"In that case, absolutely."

One perk of being in Purgatory is that Walker can transport us directly to Earth. If we were in Antrum, there would be several layers of security to go through.

I take my bright spots where I can find them.

Walker lowers his head. Another low hum fills the air as a large door-like hole appears once again inside the stables. Stepping into a ghoul portal feels like tumbling through space. I suppose it must be what the humans enjoy about their skydiving. I find it gets the adrenaline pumping. I do need to stay connected to Walker while in the portal, though, or I'd never find a way out. Even I have my limits on adrenaline spikes.

Walker and I step across the stable floor, hold hands,

and walk through the portal. Moments later, we emerge onto a nighttime landscape on Earth. Around me, rolling hills converge on a small valley. Hundreds of warriors line the hillcrests, their silhouettes outlined in the moonlight. Below me, the grounds are well kept; short grasses cover everything in sight. Picnic tables also dot the lower landscape, along with the odd swing set. The thin moon hangs in the night sky.

That's it. The Archer's Moon.

Clearly, this is a human park of some kind. Based on the fact that there are no mortals to be seen, I'm guessing this is one of those areas that closes at dusk. Which means there will be no humans around to be threatened by the demon. *Good.*

Speaking of the demon, she stands at the center of the valley, wearing some kind of gingham dress that reminds me of Dorothy from that human movie, *The Wizard of Oz.* The she-demon even has a basket and some sparkly red shoes. I've never seen anything like it before. Either this is a Class F Mirror Demon—they take forms they see in culture and are notoriously easy to kill—or something incredibly sinister that's just posing as one. That's a well-known tactic for Class A demons.

Since I can't determine the class on sight, I pull out one of my charms from the House of Striga. This particular item looks like a stick of gum, but it's actually a demon detection spell. I tear off the wrapper and stare at the chewy treat inside. The words *demon type unknown* slowly appear on the treat.

Either my charms are malfunctioning or this is a rather advanced demon. Only a handful of Class A monsters could confound one of the charms from the House of Striga. Concern charges through my nervous system.

Now I don't merely suspect this might be a Class A— I know it with all my soul.

I need to find the Earl of Acca and soon. Attacking this she-demon is suicide.

Scanning the landscape around me, I see no sign of Aldred. I approach the nearest commander. Good thing I make a point to memorize all the names of Acca officers. "Bertram."

"My Lord. I didn't see you approach."

"Where is your earl?"

Bertram lifts his chiseled chin. "You're not my commander when I'm on Acca demon patrol. I have to tell you nothing."

For a man who's about to rush into a suicide mission, Bertram has absolute faith in the earl's leadership. This is all because Acca does more brainwashing than real battle training. Unlike demon patrol, the Acca warrior-training schedule is one thing that I'll absolutely be able to change when I marry into the house. It might be one of the only upsides, actually.

"Come now, Bertram. You know exactly where he is. Tell me willingly, or I'll make life back in Antrum rather uncomfortable." Mostly, I get the royal physicians to say the fighters aren't fit for duty. There's nothing worse for a warrior to be on the sidelines for a year or so.

A muscle twitches in Bertram's heavy neck. "Fine. My earl is about a half-league to our right, standing tall with his warriors." The commander lowers his voice. "Don't ruin this battle for him." He glances up toward the sky.

Bertram doesn't say anything, but I know exactly what he's thinking about here. It's what I've spent so much time researching as part of my secret plan.

The Archer's Moon.

This is one of the mysteries of the initiation into becoming a full Acca warrior. None may speak of it, but with enough research, I found out the truth. When the moon is at its thinnest phase, it looks most like the drawn string of a bow. Performing great deeds under the Archer's Moon—or even as near to it as you can get —gets your name carved on the wall of their inner sanctum. The earl almost always tries some kind of attack at the Archer's Moon. Which hangs overhead right now.

Last year, he got fifty warriors killed when they went up against ten Class B demons. I shudder to think what he has planned for tonight.

"Excuse me." I march off in the direction that Bertram indicated. Walker stays close behind. Sure enough, the earl is wearing regular infantry armor so as to blend in with his troops. However, his meaty belly makes for an unmistakable silhouette, even in the moonlight. I march right up and stand in his line of vision.

"Aldred. Call a retreat."

"Greetings, my lad." The earl laughs as if I'd told a great joke. "What a sense of humor you have. Come see this latest display of my military strength."

The muscles in my throat constrict with held-in fury. "You don't know the class of demon."

"Sure, I do. It's Class F, Mirror Demon."

"Then why kill it? Doesn't seem too harmful. And it's not attacking. It's against our code to go on the offensive without provocation."

"It provocated us before."

"Sure it did. And it's provoked, not provocated."

"Whatever. It attacked us before, and it's absolutely a noteworthy kill. A demon is a demon, my boy."

"Class A demons are very different. And they often masquerade as a lower level entity."

"Bollocks. That's a Class F. You're a coward."

Frustration heats my bloodstream. The earl is lying. It's his favorite way of handling unpleasant truths. Ignore them. Insult the one who speaks the truth. "This is an order, Aldred. Call your men off."

"I don't need to follow your orders here." His piggy eyes narrow to slits. "And if you continue to interfere with my demon patrol, I'll say you're in flagrant violation of our treaty. I have witnesses." He steps closer. "In fact, I can execute you right now, just for walking into my patrol. What do you think of that?"

If Aldred believes that he'll frighten me, he's wrong. I'm committed now and beyond caring. "I think your house has demon patrol mortality rates that are three times higher than any other house."

"Really? Three times? I wasn't aware."

I've heard the phrase *seeing red*. Now, I know what it means. Fury colors the world around me. "That's simply not true. We've discussed this on many occasions." I pull his dagger from its sheath. "And if you're going to execute me, better do it now."

"Ho, now. Don't get hysterical. Where your father?" Aldred stands on tiptoe, as if hoping Connor were waiting behind me. "He'd see the logic in my battle plan."

"Father is on his anniversary trip, so you can give up

on that ploy. Call off your troops. There are no humans here. Attacking a demon when we don't know its class is suicide."

"Gah. Look at her. She's a Mirror Demon."

Down in the valley, the she-demon in question looks up us and blinks innocently. I point in her direction. "Did you see that?"

"What?"

"That demon is listening to our every word. She just blinked up at us as if to say *what a harmless creature I am.* That's a well-known Class A trap. She's playing you like a fiddle. Class F demons have the IQ of pond scum. This one is Class A, no doubt about it."

"I'm sure you're right." The earl holds up his pudgy pointer finger. "But, in the interests of demonology, may I show you what happens when we call in a volley of bolts?"

"You've done this before?"

"All night long. I told you, she's been provocating us."

"Provoking."

"Whatever. The men are nearly out of bolts for their crossbows. This she-demon has a rather interesting reaction."

I scan the warriors more carefully. The Acca fighters all stand in neat rows. *Battle formation.* All of them grip a crossbow in their hands. That's fine. If the she-demon could attack from this far, she would have already, so crossbows are a safe play. They're also Acca's specialty. It's hand-to-hand combat where things get tricky.

"Then go on." It's always good to learn about new demonic reactions to our weapons.

The earl steps forward, raises his arms. "Prepare for Acca Assault Plan Seven!"

I raise my hand, palm forward. "I'm not aware of that one. All assault plans are supposed to go through me." And I only assign Greek letters to them, such as Assault Plan Alpha. Yet another example of the earl being a pain in my backside. If you give warriors on the battlefield the wrong assault plan number, things get dangerous, fast.

"Damn those messengers of mine. Must have forgot to send the new plans your way."

Fresh waves of rage roll through me. "Aldred, stop lying."

"No worries, my boy. Soon we'll be family, right? It's all part of what fathers do for sons."

The thought of Aldred as my father-in-law makes a nasty taste fill my mouth. I push the thought aside. The marriage is necessary simply because Adlred is so foul.

Aldred claps his hand on my shoulder. "I can be generous. I'll not execute you for interfering with my demon patrol this time. And I'll even make sure the plans get to you soon." The earl turns back to his warriors. "Begin!"

Along the hilltop, the warriors raise their crossbows. Moving as a single unit, they aim at the she-demon.

After that, they fire.

The bolts reflect moonlight as they zoom toward their target. Instead of striking the monster, the bolts pass right through her. *Interesting.* Mirror demons can turn transparent at will, so bolts passing through it is no surprise. However, the way they turn transparent is very particular. Weapons pass through them without seeming to have any effect. That's not what's happening now with this particular she-demon. As the bolts pass through her body, there are concentric ripples—like the effect of water droplets on a still pool. My mind spins through everything I know of demon lore. I can almost place the effect, but not quite. A lead weight of foreboding settles into my stomach.

"That's quite a response," I say. "She isn't transparent so much as—"

The earl grabs my shoulder. "Quiet now. Here's the good part."

On the battlefield, the warriors begin to race toward the demon. A chill rolls through my insides. "You said that your warriors would just fire on her."

"Projectiles followed by hand-to-hand combat. That's Acca Assault Plan Seven."

Worry spikes through my limbs. "Hand-to-hand combat with a Class A? They'll be murdered. Hold them back! Stop them now!"

Aldred rolls his eyes. "I told you, she's not Class A. She's a Class F mirror demon."

But the warriors are already charging down the hill-side toward the she-demon. Even worse, they're still shooting darts as they go. My stomach drops. This is one of the critical gaps in Acca's training. These warriors simply don't know hand-to-hand combat, which makes racing toward a Class A demon even more dangerous.

I step forward and raise my arms. "Warriors of Antrum, your future king calls to you. Stop!"

Sadly, the Acca fighters don't even slow down, let alone stop. If anything, the manic gleam in their eyes shines more brightly. When it comes to battle, they only follow the earl.

This won't end well.

Beside me, the earl grins. "They won't listen to you. These are my fighters, and they value their autonomy." He rubs his meaty palms over his round belly. "I'm so glad you're here. All this worry about mortality rates and needling me over who leads my own troops. Watch now. See how well I handle them in this battle. That one little she-demon is as good as dead."

The warriors close in, and that's when the she-demon changes.

What was a mirror demon now takes the form of a hulking male demon with stout legs, six arms, and a porcupine-like collection of spines along his back. Every inch of the demon is covered in dark plated armor. Its eyes flash red.

That's bad enough. What happens next is even worse.

The demon then slices off into a series of two-dimensional cuts. These are dozens of paper-thin version of the same monster. My heart sinks.

That's a Soul Slasher.

These Class A demons break off into paper-thin versions of themselves. After that, the two-dimensional monsters cut through their prey. Soul Slashers don't cause any physical damage, but they do murder their target's spirit. And without a soul, the body dies as well. *Painfully.*

My heart rate spikes as I turn to Walker. "Portal me in there."

Walker sets his hand on my shoulder. "It's already too late."

Suddenly, the valley is covered in paper-thin

versions of the Soul Slasher that cut through hundreds of warriors at once. Acca warriors crumple on the battlefield; their howls of agony reverberate through the night air. Every corner of my soul echoes with their pain.

"Take me in anyway," I tell Walker. "Behind the first version of the Soul Slasher."

Walker gives me the barest of nods. He's a warrior, same as I am, which means he knows what I'm planning. Walker pulls out two daggers from his ghoul robes.

Smart move, Walker.

I pull my baculum from their holster at the base of my spine. I carry these weapons with me always. Baculum look like two small silver rods, but since I'm from the House of Rixa, I can ignite them with angelfire in order to create any kind of weapon.

And Walker is right. Daggers are the best choice for a Soul Slasher.

Walker then opens a ghoul portal, which we both step through. A moment later, we march out once again, emerging right behind the original place where the Soul Slasher first stood. Bodies of Acca warriors litter the valley around us. A hundred paper-thin versions of the Soul Slasher hover above the corpses. Moving in unison, all the versions turn toward their new target.

Walker and me.

Perfect.

This isn't my first time in battle with Walker. On reflex, we move to stand back to back and face the oncoming horde. Some small part of me screams that this is suicide. More of me is enraged at the loss of so much life.

I will end this demon or die trying.

The paper-thin Soul Slashers rush at us in a great shimmering wave. At this angle, they seem like a hundred full-bodied Souls Slasher monsters, but if you could view from the side, you would see that each is barely there.

Doesn't make them any less deadly.

Soul Slashers are easy to kill, but only if you strike them with a dagger at precisely a sixty-six degree angle. I ignite the baculum rods in my hands into two daggers made of white flame and wait.

Sixty-six degree angle...sixty-six degree angle.

The Soul Slashers are twenty feet away.

Ten.

Five.

The first Soul Slashers get close, and I get into battle position, arms out. Behind me, I feel Walker's ghoul robes shift as he does the same. The Soul Slashers only need to pass through my body to kill me.

I tighten the grip on my baculum daggers.

One.

My mind clicks off. My world becomes nothing but demons, battle, and reaction. I make an upper cut. Parry. Slice. One Soul Slasher passes halfway through my body. Pain radiates through me. My breath catches while I cut it through on the opposite side, killing that version of the monster.

Too close that time.

My body is slick with sweat by the time we've weeded the Soul Slasher horde down to one final paper-thin version. The thing still looms massive with its spiked back and six muscular arms.

I glance over my shoulder to Walker. "Assault Plan Xi Theta?"

He nods.

With that, Walker and I race toward the paper-thin version of the demon, our every step in sync. The last Soul Slasher moves to attack as well. At the last moment, Walker and I split formation to race around each side of the two-dimensional form. As we run along, we hold out our daggers at the precise angle.

Sixty-six degrees.

The last Soul Slasher falls over, dead.

Now all the paper-thin forms rise up from the battle-ground, forming a great swirl of motion as they rejoin into the shape of a full three-dimensional monster. It's the last thing this particular demon will ever do in this world or the next. Once the Soul Slasher's body is reformed, it tumbles onto the ground, a lifeless hulk.

We killed it.

Couldn't happen to a nicer demon.

I extinguish my baculum and set the bars back into their holster. Normally, I experience a surge of triumph after a successful fight. This time, a weight of sadness settles into my bones. The Soul Slasher is gone, but so are hundreds of Acca warriors.

On the outside, I must look calm. But inside? I'm howling with rage. Dead bodies lie around me. Their forms show no physical damage, but their souls have been cut to ribbons. They won't even get a chance at an afterlife.

The earl pads up to stand beside me. He gestures across the battlefield. "Now, this is a surprise."

"You should have listened to me." My voice drips with fury. "I want the rest of your commanders on my personal training grounds tomorrow at dawn. They desperately need coaching in hand-to-hand combat."

"What? No one could have foreseen this kind of attack." Aldred's ears turn pink as his temper rises. "You can't mean to undermine my careful work with my own warriors. You're not my son-in-law yet."

"You want an inquest on this?"

"Do that, and you'd be inviting your own execution." Little bits of spittle fly from the Aldred's mouth. "You can't stop me. Interfering with my rights on demon patrol is a killing offense!"

"Don't care. Don't try me. My practice grounds. Your commanders. Tomorrow morning. A week of training in hand-to-hand combat, or I swear, I will raise an alliance of the other houses against you."

"You can try. Your father wouldn't allow it."

"My father isn't here."

A long pause follows. Finally, Aldred steps away and forces a laugh. "Bah. What can a week of training do, anyway?" He points right at me. "And only you do the training, no one else."

"Agreed." I turn to Walker. "Take me back to Antrum."

Walker bows slightly at the waist. "As you command." He winks.

"Go on," snarls Aldred. "Enjoy my leniency until your father returns. He'll talk some sense into you, and I won't be so forgiving next time!"

While Walker creates his portal, my thoughts return to my secret plan to thwart Aldred and his demon patrols, once and for all. This chance at training is a stroke of good luck. It could make all the difference when my plan does come to pass. It all hinges on the

Earl of Striga, Aldred's bloated ego, and the Archer's Moon.

But for now, there's nothing to do but wait...and visit more families of the fallen.

Two hundred warriors lie dead on this battlefield.

I can't let that happen again.

4

*T*he next morning, I wait for the Acca warriors to arrive on my personal practice grounds. This area is nothing special really: a wide swath of yellowing grass that's ringed by browning woods. As always, gray skies loom overhead. In that way, Purgatory is a lot like Antrum. You'll never see even a sliver of blue sky in either place.

I sense the Acca warriors before I see them. Through my own feet, I feel the slight rhythmic thump of their boots on the ground. Some telltale crinkling of leaves and crackling of branches as they march through the forest. My heart rate quickens.

Today is a chance I simply can't pass up. I plan to challenge Aldred to a fight under the Archer's Moon. If I win, I can claim any boon that I wish. Chances are,

Aldred will have me battle one of his commanders instead. I don't have long to learn their tricks.

Twenty Acca warriors march out from the tree line in two neat rows. I approach the first commander in line, a hulk of a man that I recognize instantly. "You're Lothar, correct?"

"I am Lothar the Fierce." His deep voice carries the heavy accent of someone who grew up on the outskirts of Acca territory. It's a cross between the gruff sound of human German combined with an American hillbilly twang. "My earl trains me. We should not be here." Lothar glares. "Our house has treaty with yours. You no order me around."

"And yet you're here," I say. "And on your earl's orders, no less."

For a moment, Lothar's lips hang open as he debates what to do next. Then he snaps his mouth shut.

Smart move.

I gesture toward the empty practice field. "Why don't we start training with you, Lothar?"

"I no need training. I show you." The hulking man reaches into a thigh pocket and pulls out a dart. "I pick it up and throw it." With a powerful flick of the wrist, Lothar chucks the dart into the trees. Somewhere in the shadows, a small animal shrieks.

I lift my brows. "I believe you just killed a cat."

"No cat. Squirrel." Lothar taps his temple. "I know how to fight, get it?"

This is too rich. "Lobbing darts at squirrels does not equate to prowess in hand-to-hand combat. And close fighting, my dear Lothar, is why you're here."

"You no understand." Lothar reaches for his pocket again and pulls out another dart. He carefully slips the covering off the needle-like ending. "This one has poison. I hold in my fist and punch you in the face. You die. Hand-to-hand combat is over."

I nod, impressed, and store away that fact for the future. "I must admit, that's one battle tactic I didn't realize you employed."

"Good. We go."

"It doesn't change the fact that hand-to-hand combat is a lot more than sneaking out a poisonous needle." I rest my hand on Lothar's arm and lower my voice. "You know what happened with the Soul Slasher."

A pang of hurt flashes in Lothar's eyes. "I do." He recaps the dart and sets it back into a pocket on his training armor.

Good. He's listening.

"How would you stop the next Soul Slasher?" I ask.

Lothar frowns. "I pick it up and throw it. That's what my earl says." The statement lacks the mindless conviction he spoke with before, though. I consider this major progress.

"Well, Aldred is not here." A rhythmic *crunch* sounds from the forest line. I don't need to turn around to know that someone's stepping onto the practice ground behind me—and this particular someone has a very distinct tread. "Correction, your earl just decided to join us." I turn to face him. "Good morning, Aldred."

The earl scans the practice grounds. "Where's Connor?"

"Did you forget? It's my parents' anniversary. They always take a small trip to celebrate." It's one of my favorite times of year, actually. I get a lot of schemes completed in their absence.

"Be that as it may," huffs the earl. "I'm here to round up my warriors."

Aldred is many things, and predictable is one of them. I knew this was coming, but I feign a small look of surprise. Never let your enemy know you can read them. "But the warriors only just arrived. As you recall, we agreed to a full week of training."

"That's far too long. I don't remember anything like that."

"It seems we have a disagreement of history. Shall I order the Earl of Striga here? He can cast a binding spell and hold us to our respective promises." I step closer. "The agreement was for a week, Aldred."

In truth, I have far better things to do than spend a week with Acca's commanders. That said, I had to ask for a week. If I had requested a day of training, then Aldred would never shut up until I cut it down to an hour. This way, I ask for a week and get the day I actually want. Win-win.

I snap my fingers, as if an idea is just forming. "I'll make you a bargain. How about I release your warriors after one day's training?"

"Agreed."

"But I have a condition."

Aldred waves his hand. "Name it."

"I need to make sure your commanders have retained what they've learned. I'd like a display of their new skills, right here."

Aldred puffs out his jowls. That's his classic negotiating tell. It means he's interested but not convinced. "A display, eh?"

"Surely. I'll hand out honorary ranks in the royal military for those that pass the tests That way, we can make it a celebration, if you like. I'll provide the mead and roast meats."

Aldred is nothing if not notoriously cheap. "You will?"

"You have my word."

"In that case, yes."

"Excellent. The festivities can start on Saturday at sundown."

"That's three days away. Why the wait?"

"They need time to practice, don't they?"

"I suppose." Aldred purses his lips. "Hard to have a display of prowess in the dark, though."

"But better to enjoy mead and food." And enact my plan, not that I'm sharing that part. "Besides, my parents plan to return from their trip on Saturday night. They'll able to join us."

"Ah, yes. Connor will be back." Aldred rubs his rounded chin. "Yes, that's a capital idea. I have a lot to discuss with him, you know."

"I do know." The thought settles on my shoulders like a lead weight. Both my parents will be less than pleased about the incident with the Soul Slasher. "Until then." I gesture back to the tree line. "If you'll excuse us."

"Of course, my boy." A sneaky gleam shines in Aldred's mismatched eyes before he turns off to march back toward the woods. He'll lurk in the trees and observe us, no question about it. Still, it's the point of the thing. Lurking is where he belongs.

I return my attention to the soldiers. "Let's get to it. We have a lot of work to do in one day."

Before me, Lothar finally picks up a practice sword. In my heart, a choir of angels sings to celebrate the moment.

I pick up my own wooden sword and work hard not to smile. The next stage of my plan is set in motion.

Battle training is about to begin.

The day of training passes quickly. It seems like only a few hours go by before the skies in Purgatory darken. To be sure, this place is always cloudy, but I'm starting to sense that deeper hue of charcoal that means night is about to fall.

I do keep my word. Aldred and I agreed to one day of training. I dismiss the commanders. Within seconds, they are marching off the practice grounds in their neat rows. When it comes to projectiles and synchronized marching, no one is better than Acca.

Once they're well and gone, I leave the practice grounds myself. After a full day of training the Acca commanders, every muscle in my body has that pleasant ache that only good battle training can deliver.

I march down the quickest path to return to my

cabin. The browning leaves arch overhead, appearing darker against the fading light. There's something comforting about dusk. I pull a rotted leaf off one of the trees and twist it by the stem in my fingers. Like all things in Purgatory, it's dying. A latticework of holes has been munched through the leaf by some insect or two. The pattern is intricate, almost beautiful.

The thought makes me stop.

I might actually be starting to like it here.

All of a sudden, Zachary bounds around a turn in the path ahead. He's wearing cotton trousers and a black tunic, so the boy isn't on duty. He stops before me, all knobby knees and panting chest.

"Your Highness, the Doxy demons are back."

"They come back regularly."

"But these are Arch Doxies."

"Are you sure?"

"Yes, they have red bodies and everything. I was just going to alert my commander when I saw you."

Arch Doxies are a Class C demon, mostly because their bites can be incredibly poisonous. "You did well. Please alert your commander."

"But I want to go with you."

"If you were my son …" I pause, trying to picture what kind of child I'd have with Lady Adair. I don't know her well, but I do know that house. I shake my head, forcing my thoughts back to Zachary. There's no point thinking negative thoughts about my impending marriage. It's an arrangement and I shall do my duty. I clear my throat. "Fighting Class C enemies is no place for a young boy."

Zachary's thin shoulders slump with disappointment. "As you say, Your Highness."

"Why don't you go see Cook? Tell him I said you can try some of those cloud-side desserts he was able to buy. Twinkies, I think they call them."

"Really?" Zachary works hard to hide his delight. "I mean, if you're sure."

"Positive. You did well, and one day you'll be fighting Doxies, I assure you."

"All right. Thank you, Your Highness!" He runs off a few steps and pauses. "Maybe you'll see the girl this time."

"The girl?" On reflex, my hand goes to my breast-plate. I still keep Zachary's drawing there.

"Yes, the one I told you about before. Maybe she's back."

I ignore the way my pulse speeds up. Zachary is a talented artist who drew a lovely mystery girl while under some kind of spell—not that my enchantment breakers have found any signs of magic on him yet. Still, what are the chances that there really is a phenomenal female thrax warrior in the stables right now ... and one that I've never heard of, let alone Mother? The Queen has a keen interest in developing female warriors, along with a spy network to discover if any actually exist. The fact that one would be running around Purgatory without Mother being aware? Not likely.

"Understood. Thank you, Zachary."

As Zachary runs off, I head toward the stables again.

No matter what fantasy Zachary drew, the realty is that it's next to impossible for a female thrax warrior to be anywhere near this compound. And that thought makes me far sadder than it should.

I take my time entering the stables. Night has fallen more deeply, but there's still enough light to see by the naked eye. It's not often that I get a chance to take on demons solo. Most of the time, I'm leading a patrol and using the mission as a way to coach other thrax.

But a chance to kill demons alone and with abandon? I plan to savor this.

I step inside the dimly lit stables. Immediately, one thing is clear. There are Arch Doxies everywhere. They have the classic look of the breed: wide faces, horned heads, bat wings, and serpentine bodies. Dozens of them fly about the main aisle of the stable. More scurry about the floor.

The horses are wide eyed and terrified; their marble eyes seem ready to pop out of their heads.

I stick to the shadows by the main doorway and consider my options. There are too many demons here for a direct assault, especially considering how I'm in training gear versus battle armor. Arch Doxies may be frightening to horses, but they are incredibly poisonous to humans. One too many bites, and I'm done for. So I need some way to group them up and get them out of here. But how?

Suddenly, I notice a long horse tail moving along the central aisle of the stables, seemingly on its own. Kneeling down, I get a closer look at the item. In fact, it's actually a lure made from strips of horsehair fabric. Some thrax warrior is drawing the demons away. *Clever.* Even better, the scent of cinnamon hangs heavy in the air. That particular smell is ambrosia to any kind of Doxy.

On the opposite side of the stables, a figure moves in the shadows. It's as Zachary said—this is someone in ghoul robes who certainly isn't a ghoul.

The false tail winds down the main aisle. A heartbeat later, all the Arch Doxies flock to the lure, locking their clawed feet into the fabric while their wide mouths gnaw on it with gusto. The lure won't last long at this rate, but it will still get the Arch Doxies outside. From there, the demons will be easier to fight than in a cramped space.

Another gate swings open at the opposite end of the stables; the fighter must be leading them outside.

Damn, I wish I'd thought of that.

An image pops into my mind. It's the girl from Zachary's drawing. What if she really is here and a warrior to boot? *Wishful thinking.* Aside from Mother, the desire to fight has left this generation of thrax ladies.

No point getting overly excited about this. It's definitely a thrax man.

The thrax warrior gives the tail lure a flick, as if trying to shake the Arch Doxies off. They respond by clinging on even more tightly. *Smart.* After that, the warrior races out of the back of the stables, trailing the lure behind. The lure is almost gone, but the plan has worked. Dozens of Doxy demons stream out of the stables to follow the fighter into the darkness.

After hours of training noble Acca commanders on the basics of swordplay, this warrior intrigues me. I can't wait to see how he ends these Arch Doxies.

I take off after the fighter at a run.

6

*T*he warrior speeds through the darkened forest. I follow along, careful to stay hidden. The Arch Doxies give up on the lure and instead cluster around the fighter. Bat-like shrieks fill the air. My insides twist with worry. Arch Doxies only make that noise when chomping into their prey … And every bite is laced with deadly poison.

My breath catches. With that many Arch Doxies? That fighter doesn't have long to live.

The warrior takes off at a run; the cloud of Arch Doxies follow along. My throat constricts with concern. I push myself harder, trying to catch up. As I race along, I pull out my baculum from their holster.

Whatever I can do to help, I'm ready.

Suddenly, the sound of a great splash breaks the

night air. There's a lake nearby; the fighter must have jumped into it. Perhaps he was out of his mind with pain and poison.

My heart sinks. I can't lose another warrior.

I break through the line of trees and scan the lake proper. A coppery tang fills the air. Blood. A trail of crimson drops leads up to the water's edge. But is the blood Doxy or thrax?

Please, let it be Doxy.

I step up to the water's edge. The lake's surface stays unnaturally calm. That can't be right. There was definitely a splash.

Could the warrior have drowned? With that much poison in his system, it wouldn't have taken much to push him over the edge.

I scan the lake. It's still. No bubbles. A weight of sadness settles into my soul. It must be as I feared. Another thrax warrior is dead. And we can't afford to lose any fighter, let alone one with such knowledge of demon lore.

I cup my hand by my mouth. "Hello?"

No one answers.

"Anyone here?"

My only reply is the chittering of nearby insects.

I rub my neck and sigh. I'll need to find the Earl of Striga. He has charms and spells that can levitate a dead body from the water.

What a waste.

All of a sudden, the warrior pops out of the water. It's a girl. And not just any girl, the exact one from Zachary's drawing. Although I thought she looked lovely in the image, now she's even more beautiful in person. The mystery maiden is covered in demons and laughing.

My eyes widen. That's right. It's a little-known fact in demon lore, but water weakens all classes of Doxies, as well as nullifying their poison. How could I have forgotten? Leaping into the lake is not just clever, it's brilliant. Who knew there was a thrax woman with such knowledge of demonic lore?

Now she takes after the Doxies. Her limbs are a ballet of movement as she crushes the demons with her bare hands.

I've never seen anyone like this before. She's beautiful inside and out, and a fine warrior to boot. An electric sensation courses through my soul. How can someone like this exist, and I haven't known about her?

The girl flips around, and I can see her eyes gleam red in the darkness as she laughs. Her tail lashes behind her. The thing is covered in dragonscales. She's not a thrax then; she's a demon.

And I thought her beautiful.

Demons kill my people. I just saw a Soul Slasher take down a hundred of my warriors. What would their loved ones think if they knew that I'd ogled a she-demon?

I pull out another gum charm and tear open the wrapper. Letters appear on the treat inside, reading *quasi-demon.* Those are the part-demon, part-human residents of Purgatory. They process souls and do the bidding of their rulers, the ghouls.

So, she's a native of Purgatory. I suppose that's better than being in the same general family as a Soul Slasher, but not by much. What does it mean that I still want to embrace this girl?

The mystery girl runs off. For a long time, I can only stand and stare at the spot on the lake where she'd broken through the water's surface. One thought echoes through my mind.

Now that's a girl I could be happy marrying.

I take a half-step backward. What is happening to me? I don't know how long it takes, but I eventually find the strength to turn away and make the long trek back to my cabin. One there, it takes me a while to fall asleep, and when I do, my dreams are all the same: I picture that girl as she leaps from the water, covered in demons and laughing.

7

The next afternoon, I wait in our official reception tent for Walker. The place is filled with tapestries, tables, and benches, along with the odd vase or sculpture. It's supposed to be a place where nobility can socialize. That's why I'd already scheduled some chess-time with Walker for this afternoon. However, after what happened last night with that demon girl? Now our meeting has taken on more importance.

As a ghoul, Walker knows a lot more about Purgatory than I ever will. Surely, I will make a few quick queries about my mystery girl and then put all these obsessive thoughts to rest. Someone like me has no business spending so much time contemplating anyone who's in the slightest bit demonic. It's even worse, considering how I'm promised to Adair. A prince's duty is to his people.

At 2 p.m. on the nose, the hum of a ghoul portal sounds. A minute later, Walker steps through the door-size hole and into the tent itself. Spying me, he bows slightly at the waist. "Greetings, High Prince."

"You can call me Lincoln. We're alone, and I'm definitely casual today." I gesture across myself. Today, I'm wearing jeans and a *When Doves Cry* T-shirt. "You still want to play chess?"

"Are we alone?" Walker scans the fancy tent. "Isn't this tent normally reserved for nobles?"

"I sent them off."

"What about your parents?" The way Walker tilts his head he already knows something is wrong here. He's really too smart, this ghoul.

"My parents are still traveling for their anniversary."

Walker takes the chair across from me and eyes the chessboard on the table between us. "You have something specific to discuss."

"Not really." *Damn, why did I have to say that so quickly?* It sounds incredibly suspicious.

"I'm always up for chess." Walker tosses off his robe. Underneath, he's wearing black jeans, funky boots, and a dark T-shirt. The pale skin gives him away as undead. Other than that, he looks somewhat goth.

Walker lifts his arm and moves a pawn. I move a pawn as well. Walker shifts another pawn. I take out my queen.

"Rather aggressive today." Walker rubs his chin. "Sure there isn't something on your mind?"

"Well, you're constantly doing secret projects all over the after-realms."

Walker chuckles. "That I am."

"Do you know anything about these Purgatory demon girls?" I'd ask specifically about one girl, but I don't want Walker to think I've gotten attached to anyone. Because I haven't. I'm simply doing research.

Yes, that's right. *Research.*

Walker pauses before moving his queen. "They're called quasi-demons, Lincoln. *KWAH-zee.* And they're mostly human." He eyes me carefully. "Although to thrax, I suppose human is about as bad as a demon, isn't it?"

"We don't see the best side of humanity on demon patrol." When thrax deal with humans, it's because they've drawn some kind of demon into themselves, thanks to their own bad behavior. It's up to the thrax to get rid of the demon before they start even more trouble. "And we don't see the best side of demons, either." I shiver, remembering the Soul Slasher.

"Quasis are different." says Walker.

"Those are the girls that have tails."

"So do the men. The angel Verus is trying to put together a diplomatic ball that includes angels, demons, thrax, and quasis. Perhaps your questions can wait until you can ask the locals yourself. I'm no expert in any kind of woman."

Walker is clearly noticing my interest in the female side of the quasi population. No point beating around the bush now.

"The girls … Do any of them fight?"

Walker's hand falters; he doesn't set down his knight. It's rare for my friend to waver. Normally, Walker is an incredibly decisive player. "Depends how you define *fighting*."

"You know what I'm referring to." My pulse goes at double speed. "Are any of them warriors like the thrax?"

Walker finally sets down his knight again without saying another word. That's a response in and of itself.

"Talk to me, Walker."

"Yes, some quasi girls do fight."

"Do any of those fighters have dragonscale tails?"

"How would I know?" Now it's Walker's turn to speak too quickly.

"In other words, you do know."

Walker leans back in his chair and kicks out his legs.

"Here's the story. Purgatory is built to sort souls into Heaven or Hell. Most souls choose trial by jury."

"Got it." I make a mental note to try to schedule some Purgatory orientation training for my nobles. And myself.

"Correct, some call for trial by combat. Mostly, those are the souls who know they are bound for Hell and want to invade Heaven instead. Don't you know any of this?"

"I'm an expert in live demons, not dead humans. Please continue."

"Well, any soul with even a shred of goodness will 'go angel' once they hit Heaven. The purely evil ones won't, and that could cause no end of destruction. So, the evil souls must be kept out at any cost."

"That's why the evil spirits choose trial by combat and fight quasis."

"The battles are to the death in Purgatory's Arena."

"And both male and female fighters do this?"

Walker shakes his head. "I don't like this line of questioning. How are your marriage negotiations going?"

"Moving along." I know what Walker is hinting at: I shouldn't be interested in other women if I'm about to sign a nuptial contract. He's not wrong.

"Have you spent time with Lady Adair?"

"We danced once the other night."

"Huh. Did you actually speak?"

"You can't believe the grilling I got just for dancing. You know how my parents feel about emotion in marriage." I can't help the edge to my voice. Unfortunately, the more I learn about my mystery girl, the less interested I am in marriage to a virtual stranger. That's a problem.

"They're both very vocal on that point." Walker folds his arms over his chest. "Have you changed your mind?"

"You know me. I'm not truly interested in any girl. I'm merely asking questions so I understand the quasi population." It's a lie, but all in the name of research.

Walker chuckles. "Fine. I'll play along. What do you want to know?"

Leaning forward, I set my elbows on my knees. "What's the ratio of men to women fighters? I'm talking at the elite level, the ones who are really good."

"About equal between men and women."

"Do any of those elite lady demons have dragonscale tails?"

"Again with dragonscale tails." Walker shakes his head. "And they are quasis, not demons. I'll ask you one more time. Are you having second thoughts about entering into a marriage contract with someone you've danced with once?"

"I might be." *But not because of that demon girl.*

"Now there, I can't help you. I haven't had good luck with matters of the heart." Walker rubs his sideburns. "Let's get back to the game."

Walker and I take turns moving our pieces, but I can't process anything other than the news about quasi girls being elite warriors. I bet my mystery girl was one of those.

Walker taps his long finger on the board. "It's your move."

"It is?"

"It has been for some time."

"Maybe I'm just not in the mood for chess."

"You think?"

The image of that demon girl breaking free from the water keeps reappearing in my mind. It's like my visual cortex is stuck on repeat mode. A question tumbles from my lips before I can stop myself. "Have you loved anyone, Walker?"

"I love many people."

"That's not what I mean. Have you loved a woman? Truly loved, I mean."

"No, my history is … complicated." His voice turns thick with despair. "Not that I wouldn't like for that to happen, but love isn't in the cards for me."

"If you thought it might be possible …" I shake my

head. "I don't know why I'm babbling about this. Maybe we should just call it quits on chess."

Walker leans forward and grabs my wrist. The look on his face turns intense. "If I thought love might be possible, I'd fight for that with everything in me. I know you see the worst of the human and demon realms. You've watched too many of your fellow thrax get killed. Just … try to keep an open mind while you're here."

"That's the trouble. I can't have an open mind. I've lost my mind. There's this girl, okay? I keep thinking about her."

"A girl. A specific warrior girl. And she has a dragon-scale tail?" Walker scrubs his hands over his face. "Forget what I said before. Just focus on Adair. Get to know her for more than two minutes in a row. I'm sure you'll come to care for her. In a few months, you'll be back to Antrum."

"So you don't know anything."

"Zero." Walker seems sincere, but I also happen to know for a fact that he's a pretty good liar.

"You swear?"

Walker chuckles. "I know a lot of things, but why would I know some random quasi girl? You're not making any sense."

I slump back into my chair. Walker's right. "Apologies. I guess being here in Purgatory is making me unbalanced. I miss my home."

"It's fine." Walker rises and quickly creates a ghoul portal behind him. "We'll finish the game later, right?"

"Sure."

Long after Walker is gone, I can't stop staring at the chessboard. It's as if I'm trapped in some new kind of game, and I don't know the players, least of all my own heart.

And for a prince who prides himself on controlling his emotions, that's a rather terrifying state of affairs.

8

After Walker leaves, I start doing … things. I believe reviewing paperwork and meeting with some of the earls is involved. It's all a jumble because I'm still massively distracted.

My thoughts keep returning to my mystery girl.

That night, it takes me a long while to fall asleep. Once I finally do, you'd think I'd get some reprieve from my blossoming obsession. But my dreams take me right back to her as well. We are at a formal ball. I wear my crown, tunic, chainmail, and boots. She's dressed in a red thrax grown.

And we're dancing. With every sway and glance, more nerve endings in my body come alive. It's unlike any dance I've ever shared before.

In some ways, the dream feels so real. In others, it's

far too abstract. All my sensations are heightened. I can make out the hem of her gown. Feel her rib cage expand with each breath. Watch the candlelight cast flickering shadows over her lips.

With all my heart, I want nothing more than to kiss her.

Loud booms wake me from my sleep. Based on the shadows beyond my window shades, it's still late at night. Could there be a thunderstorm? That's awfully extreme for Purgatory. The most they get is a steady rain.

My chest aches. I really didn't want to wake up from that dream.

The booming sounds again, only far more clearly this time. Someone is at the door, and based on the loud sound of their knocking, that particular someone is quite agitated indeed. I shake my head, forcing the sleep from my mind.

Only one person enjoys pounding at my door at all hours. Aldred.

His voice soon echoes through the closed door. "I know you're in there, Lincoln. It's high time you returned my books! You've had them for days!"

I slip out of bed and pull on some flannel pajama bottoms. Sleeping in the nude is my norm, but there are some things it's better for the earl not to know. I slog over to the door and pull it open.

"Really, Aldred? Is this necessary?"

"You took those books without my permission, and now you're refusing to return them."

In principle, I never condone stealing anything, but lives are at stake here. I shrug. "And?"

"I want them back."

I start to close the door. "No."

Aldred jams his boot onto the threshold, blocking me. "Fine. Keep them."

"How very mature of you, Aldred."

"Know this. I figured out your little scheme. The Archer's Moon. Anyone can ask for a duel, and it must be fulfilled. The winner can claim any boon from me."

"You don't say." It's an effort to appear calm while my heart hammers in my throat. The Archer's Moon is indeed the crux of my entire plan. Only, I need some way to ensure Aldred will keep his word. At the very least, that means witnesses outside the House of Acca. Trapping Aldred with the Archer's Moon has become one of my more complex plans.

"Well, I'll have you know that the last Archer's Moon took place on Earth when we killed the Soul Slasher."

I raise my pointer finger. "I don't remember you taking any part in killing the Soul Slasher."

Aldred wags his thick finger at my nose. "I know

your sneaky mind. You're going to prevent my next achievement at the Archer's Moon."

"How very good of you to wake me up in the middle of the night to share that theory."

"We just had an Archer's Moon."

"I remember. It was only four days ago, remember? You murdered a hundred of your people at the event."

Aldred pulls out a small dagger from his waist. "Archer's Moon or not, if you interfere with my command again, your life is mine. Execution, Lincoln. I will do it."

"Are you threatening me?"

"It's my ancient right to protect my demon hunting privileges. No one can take that from me, on pain of death. Even you. Having you marry my daughter isn't the only way for me to gain the throne, you know."

Aldred has a manic gleam in his eyes. He thinks he has me cornered.

Not a chance.

I slam open the door, elbow him in the windpipe, and knock Aldred to the ground. "Pull a knife on me again and you'll regret it."

Aldred chuckles, and there's an unhinged edge to his laugh. "It's over. You're already dead, and you don't know it. Haven't you figured it out? You won't be able to help yourself. You'll keep trying to save my warriors, and you will step in one day and prevent my demon patrol rights. And that will be your downfall."

His words send a chill across my shoulders. "You're purposely sending good warriors to their deaths just to goad me."

Aldred slowly hauls himself to his feet. "I'll win in the end, little prince. Don't forget it." He slogs off into the darkness. With every step, the screams of those Acca warriors echo through my mind.

So many have died just so Aldred can clear his way to the throne.

If his goal was to enrage me, Aldred has done his job well. I can only hope I keep my focus enough to enact my full plan.

I'll save those warriors or die trying.

9

The days slowly tick by, and my mood doesn't improve. Three days have passed since I saw the demon girl, and I'm trying to get back to my routine.

And since my routine includes planning to end the earl's demon patrol rights, I've a very busy schedule. Everything will come together tonight, at the great event for the Acca warriors to show their prowess in hand-to-hand combat.

The logical move now would be to re-read my stolen book on the Archer's Moon, but that isn't happening. Instead, I'm running through some modern-style documents from Purgatory and—much as I hate to admit this —checking the fighting schedules of quasi Arena warriors.

In other words, the whole "focusing on my great

secret scheme against Aldred" thing is a work in progress.

Plus, these Purgatory documents are illegible. The ghouls give crazy names to the fighters. I lift the top sheet. Take this one, for example. The warrior is called Sharkey's Bane ZX-64. How am I supposed to track down someone using such an arcane filing system?

I should be more like Mother and cultivate a network of spies. Only, Mother's spies are in Antrum, and I'd need some here in Purgatory.

What am I thinking? I won't be staying in Purgatory long enough to cultivate anything but an end to Aldred killing his own people. And that's if I'm lucky.

Father slams open my cabin door. On reflex, I hide the Purgatory docs and swap them out with some traditional thrax scrolls.

"Greetings, Father. How was your trip?"

"I've been to Heaven. Spending time with your mother is better."

Normally, I try not to roll my eyes at such a statement. But this morning? There's a twinge in my chest. It feels a lot like jealousy.

Father gestures to my table. "And what are you up to this morning?"

"I'm just here, checking the latest grain mill treaties. Nothing to see." That was horrible lying, but I have no choice but to keep going. "Would you like to review some scrolls with me?"

"No, I'm sure it's fine." Father kicks the door shut behind him. "You're an excellent ruler. Your tutors would be proud." He purses his lips. "We're to have a display of Acca warriors in close combat, I hear."

"That's tonight after dark."

"There's nothing you can do to stop Acca from taking his people on demon patrol, except risk your own life in the process."

"I can make them better prepared."

"Perhaps." Father eyes me closely. "You look tired, my son. This situation with Acca must be wearing on you."

"No, I've grown accustomed to Aldred." *It's thinking about this demon girl that I'm not used to.*

"Come now, my boy. Something is bothering you."

Just like with Walker, I can't stop myself from asking the wrong question. "What's it like with Mother? She's your peer, your partner. How important is that to you?"

"Octavia is my life." A twinge of guilt darkens Father's eyes. "But you and I are different men. In your case, you don't care for silly romance. I raised you that way. You're a warrior, through and through. Trust me, we all need your marriage treaty with Acca. It's ..." Father tries to say more, but the words don't come. He does that sometimes, especially when it comes to discussing my marriage. On any other topic, I can get him to share every detail.

Normally, I trust him completely.

For the first time, I'm wondering if I trust him completely when it comes to this treaty.

Father stands and picks up the scroll once more. "Will you do your duty by your people, lad? Being in the line of succession to their throne gives us a lot more control over Acca. You won't stop Aldred from leading demon patrols, but there are still many other things you'll be able to change. Trade treaties. Training schedules. How and when justice is dispensed. It's a big step forward."

"When the time comes, you know I'll do my duty toward my people." Some small part of me points out that what I said wasn't exactly a yes. *"Doing my duty toward my people"* could be interpreted as any number of things.

Does this have anything to do with my mystery girl?

No, I'm merely giving myself options, that's all. People just don't look at someone leaping out of a lake and fall in love with them. Especially not people like me. Who cares if she's the first woman warrior I've met outside of my own mother? And sure, she may be beautiful and have an enchanting laugh, but that's not enough to really catch my interest. I'm a warrior, first and foremost. Being in Purgatory has simply muddled my mind for a short period of time.

Father pats me on the shoulder, breaking up my thoughts. "You're doing the right thing, lad." He speeds out the cabin door, no doubt on a mission to find Aldred.

Father thinks I've committed to a marriage with Adair. I've just made plans for my marriage. So why does that thought make me feel as if I've planned my own funeral?

10

I can't focus on those documents anymore, so I decide to go check on Nightshade in the stables. She glares at me as if to say, *I know why you're really here.*

Unfortunately, we haven't seen any sign of Doxy demons for days. Most likely, the whole company of Doxies should return and soon. And yes, I'll be waiting, but not really to hunt demons, even though I am a demon hunter. How crazy is that?

I'm brushing Nightshade's coat for the tenth time when I hear Mother's light footfall enter the stables. She pauses in the main aisle.

"Greetings, my son."

"Welcome back, Mother."

"Odd to find you in the stables this time of day."

"I need a break." With every passing day, my obsession with the mystery girl grows ... And more of the color drains out of my world. I sigh. "This spot is soothing."

Mother stares at me with such intensity, I swear she can see my soul. "You're waiting here for Adair. We talked about emotional attachments, Lincoln."

I brush Nightshade with a little too much force. "I don't know what you're talking about."

"So someone other than Adair. That could be tricky. What house is she from?"

"Stop this, Mother. I haven't met anyone." And the fact that saying that makes my heart thud against my rib cage? That's merely coincidence.

"Which means that you don't approve of your own choice, then. Is she from one of the lesser houses? I'd have heard something."

"I'm sure you would have."

"It couldn't be one of the Purgatory quasi-demons."

I pause. "You've been talking to Walker, haven't you?"

"He would never willingly share one of your confidences."

"Emphasis on the word *willingly*." No one is better at grilling people for information than Mother. I toss the brush aside. "You've been misled. I would never fall in love with a demon. I'm a demon hunter. Killing their kind is what I do."

"So you *do* have feelings for Adair."

"I barely know her." I turn and focus my full attention on Mother. "You've just spent a romantic trip to celebrate your anniversary. That's something I'll never have." Images flicker through my mind. A red dress. A full mouth. The dance of all dances. Only trouble is, it was a dream dance with a mystery girl. *That's something I'll never have in real life.* When I speak again, my voice comes out as a whisper. "I'm not made of stone, you know."

Mother's mouth falls open for a moment, but she catches herself quickly. "We put a lot of pressure on you."

I pick up a brush and start re-brushing Nightshade's already perfect coat. "I'll be fine, Mother. I always am. Just give me a little time to sort things through."

"Of course," Mother turns, starts to leave, and then pauses. "One last thing. Tell me about your Acca display of prowess event tonight."

"What about it?" I keep brushing Nightshade and avoiding eye contact. If Mother sees my face now, she'll know I'm hiding something.

"Please. I know you're up to something, Lincoln."

Then again, she may figure it out without looking at my face at all.

"I've narrowed it down," continues Mother. "Either you have a new romantic attachment or a possible scheme to stop Aldred from leading demon patrol."

It's on the tip of my tongue to say that Aldred lost another seven warriors last night. I just saw the reports come in not an hour ago. However, that would only confirm to Mother that I'm scheming to keep Aldred from leading his troops. Instead, I keep brushing Nightshade and not answering.

"You're not going to give me any additional clues, are you?" asks Mother.

"I know how you like a good mystery." My limbs tighten with worry. I can only hope she doesn't crack this particular mystery. She'd shut my plan down on the spot.

"That I do. I'll see you tonight, my son."

I turn and give her a goodbye wave. "Looking forward to it, Mother."

Mother leaves the stables, and I try to focus on tonight's event. Everything has to go off perfectly, or I could very well end up dead. However, images of that mystery girl keep appearing in my mind, distracting me.

And for a warrior, being distracted during a mission is never a good thing.

*a*fter Mother leaves the stables, I give up on seeing my mystery girl again. At least, for now. Instead, I try to distract myself by returning to my cabin and attempting to review the latest set of parchments from Antrum.

As ways to pass the time go, it's a terrible choice. My thoughts ping between my mystery girl and the upcoming show of prowess with Acca … and the final launch of my plan. Nervous energy hums through my veins.

This has to work.

I can't accept anything else.

Finally, it's time to hike over to my practice grounds. The light gray sky has turned a darker shade of gray, which means nighttime has fallen in Purgatory. My pulse speeds up, so I force my breathing to slow. When I walk onto the battlegrounds, it won't do to look nervous.

My path takes me through the woods. I pause on the border between the trees and the practice grounds proper. Call it an old hunting habit. A predator doesn't leap into the scene without sizing things up first.

Rain has fallen for the last few days, so the practice grounds are little better than a mud pit. A few patches of yellowing grass peep above the brown puddles, but they are few and far between. The space is ringed with free-standing lanterns, and the firelight reflects off the still pools of water. It's rather lovely.

Again, I take my bright spots where I can find them.

Long wooden tables encircle the periphery as well, their surfaces overflowing with food and mead. In the center of the green, Acca commanders stand in two neat rows. All of them wear body armor with the symbol of their house embossed on the chest; the Acca crest is a gloved fist.

Thrax in medieval garb move around the edges of the fighting space, leaving the central area open for the fighting exhibition. I count my parents in the outlying crowd along with the major earls, including the Earl of Striga.

I grin. Striga is our house of witches and wizards. That's good.

Unfortunately, there are no women here except Mother. That grates on me. Even though the crown is paying the bill, this is technically an Acca ceremony. As such, they determine the guest list … And Acca forbids women from attending virtually every fighting event.

The thought makes my blood boil. No women allowed at fighting events? That's yet another thing I plan to change once I'm in line to rule that house.

I step out from the line of trees. The Acca commanders stiffen their stance and cross their fists over their chests. It's the classic Acca salute pose, but it always reminds me somewhat of a mummy from Earth's ancient Egypt. That's what these folks seem to me right now: just so many dead men standing. That is, until my plan succeeds.

I stomp through the mud, stopping when I stand at the end of the aisle formed by the Acca commanders. All of them have crossbows slung across their backs. As I walk down the central aisle, they whip out their bows, pointing the weapons toward the sky. This part isn't typical Acca protocol. I suppose Aldred wanted to show off the new Earth-made composite bows, complete with hi-tech scope and some kind of mechanics to automatically reload more bolts.

I shake my head. Demons carry a natural amount of havoc magic that messes with anything mechanical. That's why guns are a waste of time. Those new bows may look impressive, but when it comes to demon-kind, they're actually less safe than their medieval style counterparts.

Did I mention how I want to train and equip these warriors myself?

At the end of the aisle of commanders there stands Aldred. Beside him stands an Acca page who holds a silver platter.

Interesting. I don't remember ordering any silver platters for this event. And I should know what's included, considering how I'm paying the bill.

To the right of this silver-toting page, there stand my parents. To Aldred's left are the Earls of the other Great Houses, namely Horus, Kamal, and Striga. Of these, I'm most pleased to see Striga here. I'm counting on that earl, Lucas, for some impromptu help when I need it.

Marching up the aisle, I pause before Aldred. "Greetings, my Earl."

He lifts his chin. "Lincoln."

It takes an effort not to roll my eyes. Of course, the earl knows perfectly well how to address me properly, but he chooses to use my name and not my title—Lincoln—at a state occasion. It's a blatant show of disrespect. I decide to use his Grammy's pet name for him. It never fails to drive him batty. "Good to know that we're dropping formalities, Baldie Aldie."

The other earls suppress smiles under their hands. The Earl of Striga outright grins, but then again, he's a master wizard, so he doesn't need to fear much. For his part, Aldred positively shivers with rage. I do think it's a fine look on him.

Aldred puffs out his chest. "Let's begin the ceremony."

I raise my pointer finger. "I thought there would be a show of fighting prowess before the ceremony part."

A sly look enters Aldred's piggy eyes. "Oh, I discussed this with your father. We're dispensing with the fighting and just doing the awarding of honorary titles." Aldred gestures to the page beside him. The young boy lowers the silver platter, showing how it's covered with medals.

My brows lift with surprise. "Medals? Really?" I glance over to my parents. Before, they'd seemed their normal formal selves. Right now, my father decides it's a great time to stare at his feet. Meanwhile, Mother glares at the back of his head.

"When was all this decided?" I ask.

"I was informed just a few minutes ago," says Mother. "It seems your father and the earl have been conversing about this while we were still on our trip." The way Mother says the names *Father* and *the earl,* it's obvious she isn't happy about this turn of events. If we had a royal doghouse, I'm fairly certain Father would be sleeping in it tonight.

I pick up one of the golden medals from the platter and turn it over in my hand. This one is covered in a pattern of rubies mixed with yellow diamonds. "Days? Metalwork of this quality takes months to create."

"Bah," says father quickly. "Those are just some old things we had lying about in the Rixa vaults. Thought it would be nice to put them to use."

"I see." I reset the medal onto the platter. Just one of these pieces would be worth a half-million in Earth dollars. And there must be fifty of them stacked high on the platter. My shoulders tighten as the frustration twists through my body.

How typical of Aldred. I commit to pay for a few mugs of mead, and he takes it as an excuse to raid the royal vaults.

"It's the least we can do," adds Father. "Especially considering how generous and patient the earl has been recently." He pins me with a meaningful stare.

There's no question what Father is talking about: the incident with the Soul Slasher demon. "So, the earl spared my life, and now you're raiding the royal vaults for him. Is that what we're saying?"

All the earls stare at us, wide-eyed with interest. The Acca commanders are keeping in formation—eyes front and crossbows lifted—but there's no question in my mind that they are hanging on our every word.

It's Mother who replies this time. "That's exactly what we're saying. And next time, the earl has assured us that he won't be so generous." If you didn't know my mother, you'd think her the image of calm at this moment. But I catch the slight tic at the side of her mouth. She's seething inside right now.

"It's all settled then," says Father. "Please continue with the ceremony."

Aldred then starts pulling one medal off the plate after another. It seems that none of them are, in fact, for his commanders. Instead, Aldred is awarding himself prizes. For his valor in fighting Reperio demons. For strength when confronting a rogue ghoul. And my favorite: for bravery in the battle of the evil Soul Slasher. If Aldred ever decides to wear all these medals, I doubt he'd stay upright from the additional weight.

I stand silently, allowing Aldred to get up a good head of steam before I cut him off. The earl has just finished describing how he's receiving a medal for courage in the face of obstinate nobility, when I raise my hand again.

"Excuse me," I say.

Aldred flashes his courage medal at my face. "Does this bother you? I didn't say *what* obstinate nobility I'd faced. It could have been anyone, you know. Don't assume I meant you, although I certainly could have." He laughs too loudly. "And besides, your father approved all these titles."

"That's not what I was about to comment on." When I speak again, I take care to use a loud voice that carries across the practice grounds. "I should like to challenge you to a battle under the Archer's Moon. If I win, I can receive any boon of my asking."

"Boon?" asks Aldred.

"Yes, and the boon I request would be for you to end all claims to rights over leading troops into battle in general, and demon patrols in particular."

A long pause follows with a silence so heavy, I can almost feel it press onto my rib cage, making it hard to breathe.

"Don't you have anything to say?" I ask.

"Archer's Moon." Aldred rolls his eyes. "I don't know what you're talking about."

I hitch my thumb toward my cabin. "As you know, I have the book from your archives that spells it all out. I can bring it back here, if you like. A challenge under the Archer's Moon cannot be refused. If I win, I can request anything at all, and you have to grant it."

Aldred puffs out his cheeks, which is a sure sign that he's thinking things through. His eyes darken when he realizes there is no way out of this. "Come to think of it, there is such a rule about the Archer's Moon."

"Glad we both remember it the same way."

Aldred points right at my nose. "But as we both know, the Archer's Moon took place days ago, during the battle of the Soul Slasher demon. I'm afraid your opportunity to cause me trouble has passed. And I can assure you that before the next Archer's Moon, I'll have that silly rule changed." Aldred returns his attention to the silver platter. "Now, for my next medal—"

"One more thing," I interrupt.

"What now?" Aldred's jowls jiggle with anger. "You're being rather rude, you know. I should get another medal for having to put up with you."

During our lives, each of us can claim very few moments of pure joy. One of mine is about to happen. My heart soars as I speak these next words. "You're mistaken. The Archer's Moon is above us now."

Aldred pauses, his hand halfway to the silver platter. "No, it's not." He scans the gray skies, searching for the status of the moon.

He won't see the moon, either, which is all part of my plan. Too many clouds, as always.

"Purgatory is always cloudy," I explain. "Here, you'll never see the status of the moon by simply checking the sky. And since the moon appears on different cycles here, it requires other means to check its status."

Aldred frowns. "Who thinks of things like that?"

I rock a bit on my heels. "Who, indeed?"

How I love it when a plan moves forward like clockwork.

I gesture toward Lucas, the Earl of Striga. "As the leading wizard in our lands, would you mind casting a quick spell to show us the state of Purgatory's moon?"

Lucas shares my resentment of Aldred, on the sly, of course. The Earl of Striga steps forward. "As you command, my Prince."

Like all witches and wizards of Striga, Lucas wears long purple robes with the insignia of a pentagram woven on his chest. Long gray braids trail down his back, the length decorated with beads of spell achievement. He lifts his hands under his chin.

"One." He releases a slow breath over his open palms.

"Two." Another breath.

"Three." This time when Lucas exhales, his breath comes out as rings of purple smoke. *Magic.* The mist congeals onto his palms, taking the form of a lilac-colored dove. Lucas lifts his arms, and the dove flies off toward the skies.

Aldred folds his arms over his chest. "Is that it?"

Lucas tilts his head, making his dreads clink together behind him. "Give it a moment."

The magic bird soars higher, its small form disappearing into the clouds. For a moment, it seems as if nothing will happen.

Then, a single point in the sky takes on a purple hue as well. From that one spot, the affect spreads out in concentric waves until the entire sky seems to be lilac-colored.

"You'll scare the locals," huffs Aldred.

Lucas sniffs. "I'm not a first-time mage. Only we can see this spell."

The clouds grow thinner, the purple color fading into a single sheet of night sky. And there, hovering above our heads, hangs a thin moon.

An Archer's Moon.

Aldred stomps his foot. "I know the status of the Archer's Moon on Earth, like every self-respecting member of the House of Acca. But why would I care about Purgatory? The people here are all demons that we aren't allowed to kill. It's a wasteland for our kind, so why would I know if its moon moves on a different cycle? This is ridiculous."

I focus on Aldred. "So, I take it that I've proven this is indeed an Archer's Moon?"

The Earl of Acca narrows his eyes for a long moment. After that, his gaze widens. I know that look on Aldred. He's come up with some way to turn this to his advantage … or so he thinks. "Yes, I am convinced. I accept your challenge."

"Excellent." I turn to Lucas. "You may end the spell."

"As you command." Lucas claps his hands. The sky returns to a purple color before returning to its typical sheet of gray.

I pull my baculum from their holster at the base of my spine. "Shall we?"

Aldred's mouth twitches with a grin. "What did you say to me at the battle of the Soul Slasher? I have conditions."

This is to be expected. Aldred would never fight me directly. I scan the faces of the Acca commanders. I wonder which one he will he choose to fight in his place.

"Name them," I say.

"You must fight my commanders."

"Which one?"

"All of them."

I frown. Perhaps I didn't hear him correctly. "Did you say all of them?"

"Yes, Acca tradition allows for multiple combatants, so long as they are all in the same fighting ground. And I name *all* my commanders."

My breath catches. All his commanders? I hadn't expected that move. It can't be legal. My mind spins through everything I know of obscure Acca house laws. "There's no law that states you can do that."

"True. But there's no law that says I can't, so I just made it up." Aldred picks up another medal from the platter. "That's another one of my rights, you know."

Father pipes up. "He can make laws on the fly, so long as they don't contradict current house legislation."

I glare in my father's direction. "Thank you for clarifying." I've felt frustrated with my father before, but never anything like the all-consuming mixture of rage and despair that consumes me now. For his part, Father has the decency to stare at his boots once more.

How can I do this without my parents' support? I look over to Mother. She still has that damned tic by her mouth, but she isn't saying anything, either.

Aldred exhales a long-suffering sigh. "Let us now return to the real ceremony. If there are no further interruptions, I won't even execute young Lincoln for trying to take away my demon patrol rights." Looking at me, he raises his pointer and middle fingers. "That's two times I'll have spared your life in one month. Don't forget it."

I don't know what to say. This is some kind of nightmare. Standing in front of all the earls and Acca commanders as my family kowtows to Aldred. Perhaps I should simply give up. If the Acca commanders don't seem to care about their own lives, why should I?

Aldred returns to awarding himself medals. The practice grounds take on a dream-like sheen. Memories from the Soul Slasher demon ricochet in my mind. I picture the innocent-looking she-demon. How Aldred summoned his warriors to charge. And the pitiful screams from the Acca warriors.

I glance over to the line of Acca commanders. Lothar is there, staring at me with a pleading look in his once-stern eyes. I can hear his thoughts in my mind, as clearly as if he were speaking them out loud.

If I give up now, his life might be next.

There's no way I can stand by and allow this to happen.

When I say my next words, I make sure to lock with Aldred's gaze. "I accept your challenge."

Aldred had been droning on. When I interrupt him again, he almost chokes. "Wait, what?"

"You heard me. I will take on all your commanders."

"And you didn't hear all I had to say," continues Aldred. "You will fight my commanders to the death."

"As of this moment, you rule your commanders but not me. You can order your warriors to attempt to kill me, but I won't do the same. As long as they are down and no longer fighting, I'll consider it a win."

Aldred waves his hand. "As you wish. It only makes success all the harder for you."

Mother marches toward us. "I've kept my peace about this fiasco, but now? You're actually sending in twenty warriors against my boy? And all of them have murder on their minds? You can't be serious."

Aldred sets his fists on his hips. "I've made it perfectly clear to both of you that my demon patrol rights are sacrosanct. And yet, not once, but twice I've let your son go. Now this is his choice. Not mine."

Mother rounds on me. "You can't do this, Lincoln." Her mismatched eyes are lined with tears. The sight makes my heart feel ready to shatter.

When I speak again, I take care to keep my voice low and gentle. "Do you really think you can talk me out of it?"

Mother huffs out a long breath. "No, of course not." She wipes her cheeks with her fingertips. "You're nothing but a bullheaded ninny."

"On that, we both agree." I pull her in a hug and

whisper in a voice only she can hear, "I've planned for this, Mother. I'll be fine."

Of course, I don't add in that I planned for one warrior, not twenty.

"You better be," she replies. "Or I'll bathe this field in Aldred's blood."

I can't help but smile. I really do have the finest mother imaginable.

Stepping away from Mother, I return my attention to Aldred. "Let's begin."

Aldred grins in a way that's the definition of the word smug. "My commanders," he calls. "Attack!"

The twenty warriors break formation, coming at me in a great mass. Somewhere in the back of my mind, I can feel part of my consciousness running through how I fought each warrior in hand-to-hand training. That section of me is weighing out the likelihood of different attacks and countermeasures based on the particular warrior.

But that stream of thought is a low hum in the background of my thoughts. What most of me can focus on is the number of warriors as they approach. My reaction to their attacks becomes instinctive response fueled by past knowledge. I can only hope it's enough to keep me alive.

The first warriors approach.

Twenty, nineteen.

I race for them, but at the last minute fall down to my knees into the mud. My momentum keeps propelling me forward as I slide between the two fighters. Once I'm close to the ground, I ignite my baculum as a pair of short swords, stretch my arms out, and slice the fighters' Achilles tendons. They fall to the ground. I follow up with a quick blow to the back of their heads.

Two down.

Next up: eighteen, seventeen.

This pair of fighters has pulled out their fancy metal crossbows. I transform my baculum into a pair of short whips and flick my wrists. The baculum-whips wind about the weapons, securing them to my line. Rotating my arms, I send my whips—and the attached crossbows —into a great arc that ends with the weapons slamming into the heads of their owners. The Acca warriors fall over unconscious.

Two more down.

Now, fighters sixteen to eleven come at me in a tightly-knit group. That's six at once. I suppose they've figured out that attacking in pairs isn't the smartest approach. I reignite my baculum, this time creating a fiery net between the two silver rods. I toss the net over the six warriors. It's made of thin strands of calcified angelfire. The net may look thin, but you might as well try to shift your weight while lying under a boulder. No question about it—those warriors will stay down for the fight.

It also means I no longer can use my baculum.

The next five warriors pause at a distance. That means fighters ten to five have figured out that I'm better at hand-to-hand than they are. *Clever.* They line up their crossbows.

Not so long ago, Zachary said I moved fast enough to catch lightning. Now, I need to see if I can do the same with crossbow bolts. I race over to one of the unconscious warriors, pick up his crossbow, and start shooting, rapid fire. I wound each fighter in the thigh as I race toward them. Once I'm close enough, I knock them out with a series of blows to their heads.

One thing I will say for these metal crossbows, they also deliver excellent club-action when you need to smack someone unconscious.

Four, three, and two leap over their fallen comrades to come at me. One tears my crossbow-club from my hands, so I'm left with no weapons.

Fists it is.

What comes next is nothing but a traditional, hand-to-hand and mud-filled fistfight. I take a punch to the ribs. An uppercut to my chin. Someone slams me so hard in my head, my ears start to ring.

For the first time, I start to consider that I could really lose my life.

Fear and adrenaline give me new focus. Suddenly, there's nothing but the impacts of fists and feet as I punch and knee-kick every warrior who dares to get close to me. Someone shoots a bolt through my upper arm. I don't even notice the pain.

When the frenzy leaves my mind, there are nineteen downed warriors on the field. All of them are unconscious. Only one is left standing.

Lothar.

This is the same warrior I spent the most time training. He's also the one who caught my gaze and inspired me to fight the nineteen others.

What will he do now?

Lothar raises his crossbow and points it directly at my chest. He seems to move in slow motion as he marches across the muddy ground. There's a cacophony of voices behind me. I hear my parents, Aldred, and even some of the earls. The warriors still trapped under my baculum net shout out encouragement.

"Get him, Lothar!"

"Kill!"

Even so, Lothar doesn't shoot. He keeps his steady tread toward me. Once we're an arm's length apart, he stops. My upper arm and thigh burn with pain. Something in my jaw feels shattered. If Lothar decides to shoot, I'm not sure what I could do.

Lothar reaches forward, grabs my wrist, and pulls it up to his shoulder. He speaks one word in his deeply accented voice.

"Pinch."

A sense of peace flows through my soul. After all this sacrifice, Lothar is now asking me to pinch the nerve that could make him pass out. He isn't even going to fight me. I apply pressure to the spot, and Lothar falls over like a sack of flour.

The moment Lothar falls, the cheering stops. Everyone seems to freeze in place, their gazes locked on Lothar, and then on me.

Pain radiates down my neck and limbs. Every muscle in my body screams with hurt. It takes a conscious effort to turn around and face Aldred. "Now," I say in a loud and clear voice. "I'd like my boon."

"Absolutely." That sneaky gleam is back in Aldred's eyes, though. He's nowhere near ready to give up. "You're injured, my lad. Perhaps we should finish this later."

I limp across the muddy field. Every step is a lesson in agony. I pause when I'm nose-to-jowls with Aldred. "We do this now."

"You've bested my men." Aldred grins a too-wide smile. "Let's have a shake, and you can have your boon."

Aldred reaches for me. A glint of thin metal shines from the hem of his tunic sleeve. Ah, I remember this particular move from my training with Lothar. Somehow, I find enough energy for one more round of hand-to-hand combat. I flip Aldred around, press his arm behind his back, and squeeze.

"Let me go!"

"Drop it."

"Drop what?"

I press harder until I hear the telltale snap of a broken bone.

"Argh!" Aldred howls like an animal, but he does drop the poisoned dart he'd been hiding in his sleeve. If we had shaken hands, all he would have needed to do was scratch me, and I'd be dead. Once the dart falls into the dirt, I crush it under my boot.

"Now, my good earl. Let's discuss this boon. You—and every Earl of Acca after you—will give up rights to lead your army in any way, shape, or form without permission from the crown."

"Sure, whatever you say." Those are Aldred's words, but I know his mind. He'll never give up control.

"I'm glad you agree." I gesture back to Lucas. "How

fortunate that you invited the Earl of Striga here tonight. He can cast a binding spell."

Lucas almost skips to our side, he's so pleased to cast this particular spell. The other earls look carefully neutral. My parents are beaming. Sometimes, I wonder what kind of leverage Aldred uses on my father. Mother and I have tried for years to figure it out. Seeing the pure joy on Father's face right now, it's clear that he loathes Aldred as much as I do. It's a mystery, but it's one that's proven unsolvable. It's certainly nothing I'll figure out right now.

Besides, I have far better things to do, like watch Lucas cast his binding spell. Despite the pain of my injuries, a warm sense of satisfaction spreads through my limbs.

I'm definitely going to enjoy this.

Lucas steps forward. Aldred takes a decided step away. "Come to think of it, I'm not feeling well myself."

"Don't worry," says Lucas. "This won't hurt. Much." He reaches into the long sleeve of his wizard robes and pulls out a handful of what looks like purple confetti. Lucas sets the confetti on his palm.

I purse my lips. *Magic confetti. That's new.*

Lucas exhales across the tiny bits of paper. The confetti comes alive, moving in a great whirl. Lucas snaps his fingers, and the small tornado of magical paper spins over to Aldred and plasters across him. He reminds me of a mummy wrapped in lilac-colored linen. It's rather bizarre and fitting, all at once.

"Repeat after me," says Lucas. "I will never lead my warriors into battle again."

"I will never lead my warriors into battle again."

A weight of worry and sorrow seeps from my bones. It's over. No more Acca warriors will die needless deaths at Aldred's hands. I exhale a long breath.

Yes.

Lucas purses his lips. "Ah, well. Might as well fix you all up while I'm at it." He waves his hand, and some of the confetti seeps into Aldred's broken arm. More of the enchanted paper flies at the Acca warriors, soaking into their bodies and healing them up. A final cluster zips over in my direction, where it attaches to my skin and sinks in as well. Within seconds, the wounds in my limbs are gone. My jaw has never felt better.

The Acca commanders all rise from the mud with confused looks on their faces. Lucas claps his hands, and the remainder of the purple confetti disappears.

I grin at Lucas. "Thank you."

"Anytime." He winks. "Care to share a cup of mead?"

I'm about to agree to the idea when Aldred starts bellowing. "Argh!" He reminds me of some kind of human pirate, only with a belly paunch and bad comb-over. "This is my celebration and it's ruined." Aldred marches over to one of the feasting tables and topples the thing over in the mud. "Everyone must go!"

As reactions go, I really couldn't have hoped for more. He really is taking this poorly. Aldred marches off the practice grounds, waving his arms as he goes. "This way, Connor!"

Across the grounds, Father kisses Mother on the cheek. They share a long look that's a mixture of sorrow, love, and forgiveness. I've seen it many times in my life. After that, Father stomps off to follow Aldred through the mud. No doubt, my father will spend the next few hours soothing Aldred's ego. All the other earls follow their king.

Mother and I are the only ones left. She's back to being the Queen of the Poker Face. There's no reading Mother's expression when she crosses the grounds to give me a peck on the cheek. "You did well, my son."

"Thank you, Mother."

Her eyes narrow a fraction. "You know what Aldred is going to want now."

"I do. The marriage treaty."

"He'll see it as a way to make your life miserable." Mother's mouth thins to a determined line. "I'm no longer certain that alliance is a good idea."

"I will always do my duty."

She shakes her head. "Sometimes, I wish you weren't so damned noble."

I grin. "I'll try to expand my troublemaking skills."

"Do that." She straightens out the folds of her black gown. "I assume you don't wish to join us with Aldred?"

"I'd rather have another crossbow bolt shot through my leg."

"Well said, my son." She turns and marches off through the mud as well.

Soon, I'm alone on the empty practice ground. I should feel happy. After all, all my plans have worked. I saved lives tonight. Months of reading and preparation have paid off.

Still, it all feels hollow somehow.

For a long moment, it's completely quiet on the practice ground. There's only me and the half-ruined celebration.

From the woods, I hear a girl's voice. "Ow, ooh, ow. Freaking Doxy demons."

My heart lightens. *Can it be?*

"Hells bells. Doxy demons, get over here. Enough already." The voice gets louder. "Ow. Bitey-biter. See the nice horsehair tail? This way, stupid. Over here, ow, fuck!"

All of a sudden, a figure steps onto the practice grounds. It's a human-ish shape covered head to toe in

Doxy demons. Even more of the little monsters flutter around the body in a whirlwind of activity.

It's my mystery girl. I know it. And Heaven help me, I could cheer for joy.

The little monsters' wing flap as she races past me, knocks over a feasting table with a very loud 'ow fuck,' and then runs off into the forest again.

I nod and smile. My mystery girl is correct; that particular path through the trees is the fastest route to the lake.

After she's gone, I stare at the spot where she disappeared. Perhaps I should follow. After all, it's part of my duty to make sure I watch an excellent warrior do her best against a demon horde.

That's right. That's all I'm thinking about. Learning some demon fighting tricks, nothing more. And once I find her, I'll merely watch her from afar. That's all. Seeing her again will ensure that all this mushy love stuff will be out of my system forever. After all, I am Lincoln Vidar Osric Aquilus, High Prince of the Thrax and I am no slave to my heart.

I can stop obsessing about this girl.

At least, I think I can.

Her laughter sounds again, and I race off into the woods. And for the first time in ages, I rush off into the unknown and smile, picturing my mystery warrior laughing and fighting. Perhaps definitions of duty can change, after all.

~

The End
The adventure continues in LINCOLN!
Read on for a sample chapter...

ALSO BY CHRISTINA BAUER

LINCOLN

The adventure continues with LINCOLN, Book 2 in the Angelbound Lincoln Series!

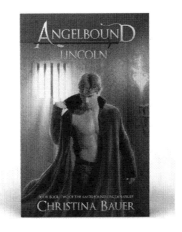

CLICK TO ORDER

ANGELBOUND

The kick-ass paranormal romance with more than 1 million copies sold!

CLICK TO ORDER

FAIRY TALES OF THE MAGICORUM

Don't miss these modern fairy tales with sass, action, and romance that *USA Today* calls a 'must-read!'

DIMENSION DRIFT

DIVERGENT meets OCEAN'S EIGHT in this dystopian adventure!

C LICK T O O RDER

BEHOLDER

Like GAME OF THRONES? You'll love the BEHOLDER series!

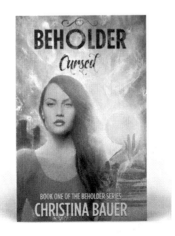

CLICK TO ORDER

*B*efore me looms a dissolus demon. Think about a waist-high glob of mayo—only both alive and deadly—and that's the general idea. No face, no limbs. It's mega-bacteria with attitude. For hours, I hunted this creature through the woods of Purgatory. Now I've cornered it in the royal stables.

All that remains is the kill.

This won't be easy.

Little by little, I pin the dissolus against the wall with my body. The white slime of the demon's exterior smears across the legs of my kevlar armor. The creature's round form pulses, heartbeat style. Reaching forward, I slip my hands through the monster's outer layer, careful to keep my palms tipped at precisely forty degrees. Unless I use that exact angle combined with slow speed, the demon's interior will transform from ugly slop into deadly acid.

Then I'll be dissolved in seconds. Painfully.

Sweat beads down my spine as I search inside the monster. My goal is to find the creature's nucleus—the equivalent of its heart—which is a solid orb about the size of a baseball. I shift my arms inside the gooey interior. Slurping sounds ricochet through the air. Across the stables, a horse whinnies. Adrenaline spikes through my system. There's a time limit here. If I don't grab the nucleus fast enough, then the demon's insides will turn acidic anyway. It's an effort, but I somehow keep my motions slow and steady. All thoughts collapse into a single goal.

Grasp the nucleus.

A familiar voice breaks up the quiet. "Interesting monster, eh?"

Seriously?

That's Aldred, the Earl of Acca and an extraordinary scumbag. He's a portly fellow, middle aged with thinning hair and long jowls. While I spent hours hunting the Dissolus, Aldred followed behind at a safe distance, releasing a steady stream of chatter. At this point, he and

I are the only people in the stables, if you don't count the demon.

"*Interesting* isn't the word I'd use," I reply.

"What can I say?" Aldred steps beside me, scanning the scene. "I'm an earl, not a walking thesaurus."

For a moment, I see myself in Aldred's eyes. I'm Lincoln Vidar Osric Aquilus, High Prince of the demon-fighting Thrax. At eighteen, I'm tall and broad-shouldered with brown hair and mismatched irises. I also happen to be leaning over a possessed blob of white goo the size of an engorged Hippity Hop.

"So, what *would* you say?" asks Aldred.

Enduring a morning of the earl's chatter (combined with seconds before I'm killied by acid) makes my last thread of Aldred-shaped patience snap.

"Two words," I reply. "Be. Silent."

Aldred raises his hands, palms forward, in a movement that says *I didn't do anything*. "No need to get testy."

Frustration sends my thoughts reeling. How did I get here anyway? The answer flickers through my mind like images on a carousel. On orders from Verus, the Queen of the Angels, my family and I are temporarily residing in Purgatory, along with all our court. Since my people enjoy a medieval lifestyle, we've constructed cabins in Purgatory's Alighieri Woods. This morning, a dissolus broke free from our royal menagerie. Cue me chasing the monster through the forest while the earl follows behind. Which brings me to the present moment and imminent death.

"This is taking too long," declares Aldred. With mincing steps, the earl creeps up beside me.

"Stay back," I warn. "That's for your own safety."

"No, I shall kick it for you."

"Absolutely not," I counter. "You'll end up losing your boot as well as your foot, and that's if you're lucky."

At last, my fingers brush against the creature's hard nucleus. *Yes!* Normally I give demons a chance to retreat before killing them. However, dissolus have the mental powers of paramecium. To them, attacking is nothing personal—it's just what they do.

Time to end this.

Tightening my grip on the nucleus, I yank with all my strength. The clear sphere breaks free from the gelatinous demon. For a moment, the dissolus quivers in place. Then—SPLASH—it collapses into a puddle of translucent sludge. The scent of rotten eggs fills the air. In my right hand, the nucleus transforms into a bright white orb before vanishing altogether. I exhale a long breath.

"And *that's* how to kill a dissolus." I shake out my palms, sending residual slop flying around.

"Glad I was here to help," declares Aldred. "We make

a great team." He moves to stand directly in the main aisle of the stable. In other words, blocking my departure. I've seen this action from Aldred before.

"Is there a particular topic you wish to discuss?" I ask.

"As a matter of fact, yes. Now that we've spent the morning together, I thought we could talk, man to man."

I tilt my head. "Go on."

Here it comes. Another discussion about my marriage contract.

For weeks, Aldred has been pestering me to sign a betrothal contract with his daughter, Lady Adair. At one time, I might have been interested. Now, not so much. The local residents of Purgatory are quasi-demons, and one of those ladies happens to be an excellent warrior named Myla Lewis. As of this moment, it's been eight days, six hours, and thirty-two minutes since I last saw Myla. At the time, she was fighting off doxy demons in a nearby lake. Her battle technique displayed the perfect combination of beauty, intellect and lethal power.

Ah, Myla.

Long story short, I'm no longer interested in signing a marriage contract. Instead, my time's been consumed with researching a certain Miss Lewis. To that end, I've learned she's fighting in Purgatory's Arena tomorrow morning. I plan to sneak into an access corridor and watch her battle from a distance. The very idea makes my heart soar.

Aldred clears his throat, breaking up my thoughts. "Did you hear what I said?" he asks.

"No," I reply. Evidently, the earl was blabbing away while I contemplated Myla. Even so, I doubt I missed anything. There's only one topic of interest to Aldred these days. My marriage. "Please repeat your statement."

Aldred makes a great show of scanning the stables. "I've news for you about Minister Devak." He narrows his eyes to conspiratorial slits. "Great information."

This is what humans call a *red flag*. Why the concern? I've been working on what I call an anti-Acca treaty. By uniting the armies of Kamal, Horus and Striga, I'll have enough seasoned warriors to make Aldred kowtow on any number of topics, including my marriage to Adair. Of all those houses, my negotiations with Minister Devak—and therefore the House of Kamal—are the farthest along.

"And?" I prompt.

"Devak's been asking around." Aldred lowers his voice. "About quasi warriors."

A chill rolls up my limbs. Can Devak be interested in Myla for some reason? When I next speak, it's an effort to keep my voice calm. "What is Devak's precise concern?"

"Wouldn't *you* like to know." Aldred smirks.

At this point, that smug grin of Aldred's tells me two things. First, the earl knows exactly what Devak is up to, and second, Aldred wants something in exchange for the information.

I stifle the urge to roll my eyes. "Name your price, Aldred."

The earl exhales a long-suffering sigh. "I might confide everything, but it's sensitive information … the kind you share with *family*, you know?"

Meaning: ink my betrothal contract and I'll tell all.

I chuckle. Aldred always overreaches in negotiations. However, what he lacks in finesse he more than makes up for in persistence. "I am *not* finalizing a contract merely to discover Devak's plans."

"Please; I never expected you to sign this very second," lies Aldred. No doubt, the man keeps a copy of the contract in the folds of his tunic along with a quill, just in case. "But perhaps you can commit to spending more time with my sweet Adair? If so, then I might feel like sharing."

Aldred thinks he's being sneaky, but I already made this decision last night. "Mother is organizing a garden party at the Ryder mansion. My plan is to request Adair's company for the event." After all, I've said all of five sentences to the girl. We may be compatible. As my parents say, passion has no place in toyal marriage. Choosing Adair is about duty, not feeling. Welcome to royal life.

Aldred rubs his palms together. "Excellent, I'll tell Lady Adair today."

"Your turn," I state. "What about Devak's interest in quasi warriors?"

Aldred bobs his thick eyebrows. "No doubt, you're aware how the court itches to hunt local demons."

My eyes widen with shock. "No, I wasn't." A memory flashes through my mind.

I'm fifteen and late for monitoring a demon patrol in the Canadian Arctic. As I exit the transfer platform, a woman's screams echo through the cold air. I race out of the ice station and onto a sheet of white tundra under a grey sky. Freezing winds batter my body. Before me, a dozen Acca warriors tear apart a Vantys, which is a deadly she-demon who's equal parts human and reptile. Aldred stands behind them, pumping his fist in the air. Fresh sprays of blood darken the snow. I race over, my young voice bellowing.

"Stop!"

But the Vantys is already dead. And Aldred's men have placed her head on a pike.

"This is disgraceful," I announce. *"We are thrax, not a mindless mob."*

Blinking hard, I try to wipe out that recollection. However, the image of a severed head stays seared in my mind. Thrax should act as ethical warriors, yet Aldred transformed them into something else. There's no avoiding the truth. With the wrong encouragement, my people can do terrible things.

And now, their baser instincts may be focused on Myla. I shudder.

"You know us thrax," continues Aldred. "We're always seeking a new challenge."

Protective energy runs up my spine. I round on the earl. "The Queen of the Angels herself, the oracle Verus, sent us here to interact with the quasi population, not hunt them down."

"Bah." Aldred waves his hand dismissively. "It's only a matter of time before some quasi marches into our camp, looking for trouble. After all, they're semi-demonic. It's in their blood. And once those quasis come after us, then we'll have to protect ourselves. It's only right."

Images of Myla appear in my mind. She did indeed sneak into our compound, but only because she was on the trail of a mutual enemy, the doxy demons. A weight of worry settles into my stomach. What if someone other than me saw her? Aldred is correct; my people would kill first and ask questions later.

"You still haven't shared specifics on Devak and quasis," I point out. "What did he say, exactly?"

"Devak's asking about Purgatory's Arena."

Meaning he's focusing on warriors like Myla. "What's his interest?"

"My guess? Arena warriors will give the best fight. Here's the thing. Maybe you and I can team up." Aldred grins, showing off his mouth of yellow teeth. "Together, we could claim the first official quasi kill."

At those words, anger zings through my nervous system. "Let me make one thing absolutely clear." I prowl toward Aldred, my voice deep as thunder. "Hunting the local population is off the table, whether they are arena warriors or not. If you or anyone else speaks of this again, I'll have you shipped back to Antrum and tossed into the dungeons." For every final word I speak, I tap Aldred on the center of his chest. "Do you understand?"

"All right." The earl forces another laugh. "No need to get sensitive."

I glare at Aldred with a look that says, *I'm done here.* "The dungeons, Aldred. I mean it."

Without waiting for a reply, I storm past the earl and out of the stables. Although Aldred runs our most powerful house, I remain the High Prince and have my limits. Hunting quasis? *Outrageous!*

Suddenly, I wish my parents weren't away on a demon hunting excursion. I'd like nothing better than to open a formal inquest, find out who's threatening quasis, and then fill our dungeons to overflowing. But starting an inquest is serious business. For the process to have teeth, my parents must sign off. And they won't return for at least four days.

Ah, well. Better to wait and do this correctly, much as I hate that fact.

All the way back to my cabin, my thoughts race through everything I've just learned: that Aldred is still pressing my marriage to Adair ... the fact that my own people might be targeting quasi warriors ... and how the entire situation could place Myla in danger. It all adds up to one terrible conclusion.

If I'm not careful, Myla might end up dead. That's not an option, so I take a silent oath.

With all my mind and body, I vow to protect the woman who already holds my heart.

I spend a restless night brainstorming ways to punish Aldred and therefore, I can't sleep. The fact that I'm about to see Myla again doesn't help, either.

Finally, early morning arrives. I slip out of my cabin, mount up my horse Nightshade, and slip away from camp. We ride across rolling hills of yellowing grass, eventually ending on the back parking lot to Purgatory's Arena. Like most things here, it's a little run down.

Fine. A lot run down.

Lines of weeks poke up through the asphalt. A few lonely car hulks sit at odd places. The arena itself is little more than a pile of ruined bricks. Moss and weeds peep out between the gray stones that make out the building's outer facade. Honestly, the place looks held together with popsicle sticks and glue. All I know is that a ghoul named IK-3 is meeting me at a back access door.

From there, I get to sneak in and see Myla. The thought is a little distracting, I suppose. Night swings her silver head back in my direction. She glares at me with big round eyes as if to say, *are you paying attention here?*

Night was around the evening Myla fought the doxy demons. I think my horse is as obsessed with Myla as I am.

"Yes, yes," I reply. "That way." I gesture and click my tongue. Night takes off around the back of the huge

Arena. Sure enough, there is a boarded-over door marked No Admittance. My contact, a night guard named IK-3 waits outside. He's my contact for all things Myla and battle-related.

Ike (he hates his ghoul name) waves as we approach. "Hey, glad you could make it." He's tall and lanky, with incredibly pale skin, which is appropriate considering he's one of the undead. Ike also has a heart-shaped face complete with freckles that somehow survived the ghoul-conversion process. He looks more like a skate-boarding human than an undead ghoul.

"Thank you for your help, Ike."

"Hey, just happy for the worms, you know." Ghouls love worms. I sent Ike a case. Yes, he's been that helpful.

Ike pushes open the blocked door. "This hallway has been under construction for years. You can watch from here and no one will know. Best-kept secret in the arena."

"Thank you."

Ike stares at Night. "You need help with your horse?"

"Night can take care of herself, right girl?"

My horse sniffs, and a plume of purple smoke comes out of her nostrils. Night casts minor spells, and this is one example. One moment, Night is there. The next? Gone.

"Whoa," says Ike. "Cool."

"Horses from the House of Striga are all like that." Striga is home to our most powerful witches and warlocks. "If you'll excuse me."

"Knock yourself out."

I step into the hallway and the first thing that strikes me is the scent of stale cigarette smoke. Seems like the best secret in the arena is rather well known. The floor is littered with cigarette butts, empty coffee cups and drained containers of cough syrup. Add in a worm farm and this would be the ideal spot for a ghoul rave.

The corridor winds a bit before opening out onto the arena proper. Pausing at the end of the passage, I lean against a stone arch that leads directly to the arena floor. Before me, tiers of stone benches loop around an oval battleground. Like the exterior, the inside of this place is a mishmash of mold, cobwebs and cracked stone. Nothing fancy, but it could be Hell itself and I'd still sneak in here. I grin.

Myla's fight starts any minute.

A low hum sounds in the corridor. *Someone's opening a ghoul transport portal.* Moments later, a dark rectangular shape appears just within the passage. Out of it steps a ghoul who's tall, lean and deathly pale. As always, the strong bone structure of his face is perfectly framed by a buzz cut and sideburns. His official name is WKR-7.

I call him Walker.

As my best friend, Walker takes it upon himself to help me avoid trouble. Today, that means using his ghoul powers to track me down. He's well-intentioned, if a little intrusive.

While Walker strides closer, the portal vanishes behind him. "How very odd," he says.

"And *hello* to you too," I deadpan.

Walker folds his arms over his chest. The long sleeves of his dark robes sway with the movement. "You're not in royal gear this morning."

"True." Usually I wear leather pants, tall boots, chain-mail and a dark velvet tunic. Classic thrax gear. "Here's the thing. Today I'm blending in with the general populace." In this case, that means sporting jeans, hefty boots and a *Purple Rain Tour* T-shirt. I also keep a small assortment of weapons hidden on my person.

Daggers. Don't leave home without them.

"Blending in?" repeats Walker. "You've the mismatched eyes of a thrax."

"And I've no tail. Don't forget that part." Like me, Myla is around eighteen years old. Unlike me, she has a long thin tail that's covered in dragon scales. *So intriguing.*

Walker narrows his eyes. "What are you *really* doing here?"

I purse my lips, contemplating. *Do I tell Walker about Myla?* So far, I've avoided sharing anything with him. Not that I think my friend will be judgmental or share my secret. It's more that my feelings for Myla are a bright spot in an otherwise grey life. Telling someone else might dilute the color. But as of yesterday, I can no longer stay silent. My own people may be hunting quasis, so Walker must know everything.

In a minute.

A little teasing is part of our bro code.

"You know I'm stuck in Purgatory for a few months," I reply. "Thought I'd catch an arena match." Purgatory sorts souls into Heaven or Hell, either through *trial by combat* or *trial by jury*. As an arena warrior, Myla fights evil spirits who want passage to Heaven.

"Arena fights are private events," says Walker. "How did you discover this one?"

"Would you believe me if I said it was a coincidence?"

"Not at chance." Walker sniffs. "You recently asked me about quasi girl fighters with dragonscale tails. Now I find you skulking around an access hallway to Purgatory's Arena, right before one such fighter will do battle."

"Me? Skulking?" I open my mouth in mock-surprise. "I'm more of a sneak."

Walker doesn't even crack a grin. "I repeat, how did you find out?"

"You won't drop this, will you?"

At last, Walker smiles. "I can wait for all eternity, if you like."

He's not kidding. Walker once followed me—silent and glowering—for three solid days because I wouldn't tell him where I hid the cough syrup (ghouls love that stuff, along with coffee, worms and smokes.) Walker didn't back down then; he definitely won't now.

"Well?" asks my friend.

Time to fess up.

"This morning's match was revealed to me after—" I look up, my mouth making silent calculations "—bribing eight different government officials, beginning with the Ghoul Minister and ending with an arena night guard called IK-3. Along the way, I even discovered a name." I can't help but smile as I speak this next part. "Myla Lewis."

Walker glares daggers in my direction. "Leave Myla-la alone."

A pang of jealousy moves through me. *Walker has a nickname for her?* When I next speak, my voice comes out far lower than I'd like. "How do you know her?"

Walker's features turn unreadable. "My people rule this land. Sometimes I help out."

"There's more to it than that." I step nearer. "Isn't there?"

"You know my kind. Lots of rules. Our regulations require that arena warriors travel via ghoul portal." Walker gestures to the walls around him. "Between all the evil souls and demons running around this place, I'm one of the few ghouls who can handle themselves."

Logical enough. Like me, Walker is a descendent of the archangel Aquila and a well-trained fighter.

"So you take Myla to her matches," I recap.

"Precisely. We barely say much beyond *hello* and *goodbye.*"

Which could be true, except for the fact that Walker never uses nicknames. Point of fact: he still calls me Lincoln, and I've known him my entire life.

My friend is definitely hiding something.

I scan Walker carefully. "If that's true, then why not tell me about Myla before? I specifically asked you about quasi arena fighters who were women."

"It's not that easy." Walker's gaze locks with mine. When he next speaks, all the seriousness in the world is etched into the lines of his face. "I'd tell you everything if I could."

Some history on Walker: He's forever getting involved in tricky situations. Binding oaths, soul saving, magical contingencies … Walker has his undead hands in every-thing. Plus, I know this particular look of his; my friend is telling the truth. He can't share when it comes to Myla.

I give him a solemn nod. "I understand."

Even so, there's no way Walker *barely knows* my girl. There's more to the story and I intend to uncover every last detail. After all, hunting beings and information is what I do best.

"Most appreciated." Walker pauses for a long moment. "And since you snuck in to watch Myla's fight, I'm guessing you haven't met her formally."

"That's correct." *And I loathe that fact.*

"Myla's part demon, so I'll also assume you won't introduce yourself either."

A weight of sorrow settles into my soul. "Correct again." Considering the situation with my people wanting to kill her, having any kind of relationship seems far from reasonable.

Walker eyes me for a long moment, then he shakes his head. "Still, I don't like this. From the little I know about Myla, she could easily be taken with you. The fact that you're lurking anywhere near her? That's simply inviting disaster. What if she falls for you and gets her heart broken? I can't allow that."

If I felt a small flare of jealousy before, that emotion

now blazes into full, white-hot envy. "And why would you care?"

"Again, not answering that."

My hands curl into fists. Clearly, my friend knows Myla far more than he lets on. *Does he want her for his own?* Closing my eyes, I force my mind to calm. Getting green-eyed over Walker will accomplish nothing. My vow is to protect Myla, even from me.

When I next speak to Walker, I work hard to act neutral. "You seem to know Myla well."

Walker shrugs. "I know the quasi people."

"If Myla and I were ever to meet, how would you suggest I ensure she doesn't…" I pinch the bridge of my nose, trying to find the right words.

"End up like you?" asks Walker.

I level him with a dry look. "Precisely."

Walker rocks on his heels, setting his long robes fluttering. I've seen this move before; my friend is in deep contemplation. At length, Walker speaks once more. "You're excellent at containing or faking emotion when necessary. If you ever encounter Miss Lewis, you should play the haughty thrax. Look down on her demonic side. She'll hate it—and you—forever."

The words slam into my heart. *Myla will hate me forever.* How could I act in such a foul manner, even if it is for Myla's benefit? My shoulders tighten with worry.

When I first saw Myla, I was surprised she was a quasi demon. I'd never met one before. But after learning more about her, things have changed. Now I don't see Myla as anything but her beautiful self.

All of a sudden, that memory appears again.

The Vantys.

A bloody head stuck on a pike.

Bands of worry tighten around my throat. It doesn't matter that Myla is an excellent warrior; no one can fight off an entire mob of thrax. Taking in a deep breath, I force my spine to straighten. *This isn't about me. It's about what keeps Myla away from harm.* And considering the recent news from Aldred, safe is where I'll ensure she stays, no matter what.

Walker tilts his head. "Is that possible, Lincoln? If it comes to it, can you play the villain to keep her away?"

"I can and will." Turning from Walker, I stare off into the empty arena. Pain radiates through my chest, sharp as a blade driving though my rib cage, and I'd know the sensation. I've been stabbed no less than thirty seven times. Even so, none of those cuts reached this level of agony.

Why does caring for someone have to hurt so much?

Stepping to my side, Walker sets his hand on my shoulder. For a long minute, my friend's all-black eyes carefully scan my face. "Oh, Lincoln," my friend says at last. "I've never seen you this miserable. You've become deeply attached, haven't you?"

For a long moment, I can't find the words to explain. Then, the truth falls from my lips on its own. "There's no one else in the world like her. Seeing Myla?" I throw my hands apart and make an explosion noise. "She blew apart everything I thought I knew. A woman fighter who laughs while taking down demons? I'd no idea someone like that even existed. Thoughts of her simply consume me."

Walker gives my shoulder a squeeze. "Perhaps you should skip this morning's match."

"And miss torturing myself?" I smile, but there's no joy in it. "Not a chance."

My friend gives me the side eye. "You won't drop this, will you?"

"As a wise ghoul once told me, I can wait for all eternity. Or long enough to make you late transporting Myla." Like the rest of his people, Walker loathes missing schedules.

At last, Walker lowers his hand. "In that case, I'm off for transport duty."

"Be safe. You carry precious cargo." My voice warbles a bit when I say that last part, and I don't care.

"I will."

Another hum sounds as Walker opens a fresh ghoul

portal. Within seconds, my friend is gone. Long minutes tick by. Eventually, the arena's emcee takes to the floor, along with a handful of workers. I count quasis, demons and ghouls in the mix. Still, there's no sign of Myla.

A realization hits me. I became so jealous, I forgot to tell Walker about the threat to Myla from my people. I pause, wondering if I should chase after Walker. *Probably not, at least for now.* The conversation should wait until I'm perfectly calm and rational. And that's not now.

Finally, a rectangular hole appears at the arena's center. My heart thuds at double speed.

This is it.

A moment later, Walker steps through the dark portal. After that, *she* walks out behind him.

Myla.

I devour every aspect of her. Long auburn hair. Soulful brown eyes. Amber skin. Lovely, feminine curves. Predatory tail. Perfection.

Once Myla steps away from the portal, her face pales. It makes sense—ghoul transport can make anyone nauseous. Every instinct I have screams for me to approach her, making sure she's all right. Gripping the uneven stone wall, I force my body to stay put. It isn't easy.

Across the arena, Walker checks on Myla. I can't hear the words he speaks, but the effect is clear. Within a few seconds, Myla stands upright again. Color returns to her luscious skin. As she recovers herself, an aura of energy seems to pulse around her.

Light.

Power.

Confidence.

She's magnetic.

The emcee must sense it too, since the ghoul decides to approach her. This master of ceremonies is an especially awful-looking character with pointed teeth and a bad attitude. Once again, my protective instincts soar. My heart demands that I place myself between the two of them. My intervention isn't needed, though. Myla's full mouth quirks with a smile as she faces off against the emcee.

I shake my head and grin. *This woman.* She's fearless. Intelligent. Passionate. Just watching her awakens something inside me—a corner of my soul which craves that same ferocity for life. All the while, her presence also soothes me in ways I hadn't even known I'd been hurting. All of it adds up to one conclusion: my waiting and scheming has been worth it.

Here she is. My Myla.

The wisp of a breeze strikes up behind me, interrupting my reverie. *That's odd.* This tunnel is a sealed off behind a heavy wooden door. What could start any wind? Turning away from Myla, I scan the darkened corridor. The reason for the change of air becomes clear.

The ghost of an elder thrax now hovers in the shadows. An ethereal breeze twists around him, making his formal tunic flutter against skeletal form. A long white beard cascades to his waist. The specter is instantly familiar.

"Minster Devak?" I ask.

"Yes, my prince," replies the ghost. "It's me."

As Minister of Alliances for the House of Kamal, Devak is my contact for the anti-Acca treaty. To be honest, it's not surprising that he's a ghost. The man as rather up in years, even for a thrax.

Devak shifts his weight from foot to foot. It's what he does when nervous. "My earl has signed the latest version of our anti-Acca treaty."

"I'm glad to hear it." *One house down, two more to go.* "Though I doubt you're visiting me from the dead in order to share that information.

"Well …. It's like this …" Devak inhales a log breath. "I've been chosen by the Tithe."

My brows lift. Not what I expected to hear.

The Tithe is an immortal thrax warlock who fulfills your greatest wish, assuming you're both worthy and part-angel. Want a pile of gold? The Tithe will make it happen. Hope your enemies will disappear? No problem; the Tithe will handle it. In return, you agree to serve him through all eternity. The Tithe began life as a sculptor, so he places your ghost inside an effigy, which is a lifelike statue of your best self. You then spend forever as a happy resident in his so-called Tower of Wonders. In my mind, it's too good to believe, but my people like the idea of a fairy godfather type who solves all their problems. Plus, in this moment, the Tithe really doesn't interest me. Myla's safety does.

"Selected by the Tithe," I repeat. "How nice." Yet as I say these words, my tone is more *ice* than *nice*. "I understand you've been asking about quasi fighters."

Devak's weathered face creases into a grin. "Yes, I was asking for information on behalf of my master. There's a particular quasi he wishes to hunt. It won't be easy, so none can intervene." The ghostly Devak stares at me pointedly, as if there's no question who he thinks will intervene. Me.

Please, don't let his target be Myla. It's already bad enough that Aldred has taken an interest in my girl. I don't need a supernatural warlock after her as well.

"And who is his chosen target?"

Devak grin widens. "The Tithe plans to hunt down the demon Myla Lewis. You must allow him to claim his quarry."

The way Devak speaks, it's as if hunting a woman were nothing more than swatting a fly. His casual tone transforms my sense of worry into something else. Pure rage now heats my blood. When I speak again, my voice drips with menace. "Why Myla Lewis?"

"She's a, uh, great warrior. That is all." Devak's smile falters. I've negotiated with this minister for years. I know what it means when Devak stutters while his grin fails.

I speak two more words, slowly and with barely controlled fury. "You're lying."

Devak grips his hands under his chin. "Please. Name your price to step down. Whatever you want, it's yours. My master must cleanse the after-realms, starting with Heaven."

"I've a scribe who does nothing but field messages from thrax who have ideas on how to cleanse the after-realms. Your friend can address his ideas to Lord Aethelgood." I had to make the man a lord, by he way. It really is a horrid job. "What I care about is my original question."

To emphasize the risk here, I reach around my back to pull my baculum from their holster at the base of my spine. These silver rods can be ignited into any sort of fiery blade. I lift the bars high.

Devak's translucent eyes light up with alarm. *Good.*

"Let's try again," I say slowly. "Why does the Tithe *really* wish to hunt Myla Lewis?"

"My new master erased all my debts," whines Devak. "Soon he'll turn me into a powerful effigy. After that, I'll live forever in comfort and ease. The Tithe asks that I secure your help here. Why won't you agree? Just look away while the Tithe hunts one quasi. That's a demon, my prince!"

If that's Devak's closing argument, it's downright awful.

"Indeed, I am your Prince," I state. "Before you ever met the Tithe, you vowed to serve my rule. Now I command you; share every last detail about the Tithe and Myla Lewis." As I speak a final word, I ignite my baculum into a long sword made of white flame…

"Now."

End of Sample

To find out more about LINCOLN, visit:
http://monsterhousebooks.com/books/angelbound-series/**lincoln**

APPENDIX

IF YOU ENJOYED THIS BOOK...

…Please consider leaving a review, even if it's just a line or two. Every bit truly helps, especially for those of us who don't *write by the numbers,* if you know what I mean.

Plus I have it on good authority that every time you review an indie author, somewhere an angel gets a mocha latte. For reals.

And angels need their caffeine, too.

ACKNOWLEDGMENTS

If you're reading my freaking acknowledgements, chances are, I should thank you for something. So, for the record: you are awesome, dear reader.

That said, huge and heartfelt thanks must go out to my husband and son for their rock-solid support. Writing means a lot of early mornings, late nights, long weekends, and never-ending patience. You two are the best guys in the universe, period.

After that, I must thank the extensive network of reviewers, friends and colleagues who helped me build my writing chops in general. Gracias.

Finally, deep affection goes out to my late, much loved, and dearly missed Aunt Sandy and Uncle Henry. You saw the writer in me, always. Thank you, first and last.

Angelbound Origins

About a quasi (part demon and part human) girl who loves kicking butt in Purgatory's Arena

1. Angelbound
2. Scala
3. Acca
4. Thrax
5. The Dark Lands
6. The Brutal Time
7. Armageddon
8. Quasi Redux
9. Aquila

Angelbound Lincoln

The Angelbound experience as told by Prince Lincoln

1. Duty Bound
2. Lincoln
3. Trickster
4. Baculum

Angelbound Offspring

The next generation takes on Heaven, Hell, and everything in between

1. Maxon
2. Portia
3. Zinnia
4. Kaps
5. Huntress

Beholder

Where a medieval farm girl discovers necromancy and true love

1. Cursed
2. Concealed
3. Cherished
4. Crowned
5. Cradled

Fairy Tales of the Magicorum

Modern fairy tales with sass, action, and romance

1. Wolves and Roses

2. Moonlight and Midtown

3. Shifters and Glyphs

4. Slippers and Thieves

5. Bandits and Ballgowns

Dimension Drift

Dystopian adventures with science, snark, and hot aliens

1. Scythe

2. Umbra

3. Alien Minds

4. ECHO Academy

5. Drift Warrior

ABOUT CHRISTINA BAUER

Christina Bauer thinks that fantasy books are like bacon: they just make life better. All of which is why she writes romance novels that feature demons, dragons, wizards, witches, elves, elementals, and a bunch of random stuff that she brainstorms while riding the Boston T. Oh, and she includes lots of humor and kick-ass chicks, too. Christina lives in Newton, MA with her husband, son, and semi-insane golden retriever, Ruby.

Stalk Christina on Social Media

Blog:
http://monsterhousebooks.com/blog/category/christina

Facebook:
https://www.facebook.com/authorBauer/

Instagram:
https://www.instagram.com/christina_cb_bauer/

Twitter:
@CB_Bauer

VLOG:
https://tinyurl.com/Vlogbauer

Web site:
www.bauersbooks.com

COMPLIMENTARY BOOK

Get a FREE novella when you sign up for Christina's newsletter: https://tinyurl.com/bauersbooks

BEVERLY
HILLS
VAMPIRE

A NOVELLA BY
CHRISTINA BAUER

Printed in Germany
by Amazon Distribution
GmbH, Leipzig